THE MAGIC IN CHANGING YOUR STARS

LEAH HENDERSON

STERLING CHILDREN'S BOOKS

New York

To anyone who has ever gazed into a starry night sky and dreamed

To my dad, who will forever point out infinite possibilities and stars

To my family, who are always by my side as I search mine out

And to Boston, my furry, brilliant friend, for leading me to one—thank you!

STERLING CHILDREN'S BOOKS
New York

An Imprint of Sterling Publishing Co., Inc.

STERLING CHILDREN'S BOOKS and the distinctive Sterling Children's Books logo
are registered trademarks of Sterling Publishing Co., Inc.

Text © 2020 Leah Henderson
Cover © 2020 Brittany Jackson

ISBN 978-1-4549-4404-1
978-1-4549-3407-3 (e-book)

Library of Congress Cataloging-in-Publication Data

Names: Henderson, Leah, author.
Title: The magic in changing your stars / Leah Henderson.
Description: New York : Sterling Publishing Co., Inc., [2020] | Audience:
   Ages 8-12. | Summary: After bungling his audition to play the Scarecrow
   in The Wiz, fifth-grader Ailey is magically transported to 1930s Harlem
   where he meets his own grandfather and legendary tap dancer Bill
   "Bojangles" Robinson.
Identifiers: LCCN 2019055928 | ISBN 9781454934066 (hardcover) | ISBN
   9781454934073 (epub)
Subjects: CYAC: Self-confidence—Fiction. | Dance—Fiction. |
   Grandfathers—Fiction. | Time travel—Fiction. | African
   Americans—Fiction. | Magic—Fiction.
Classification: LCC PZ7.1.H462 Mag 2020 | DDC [Fic]—dc23
LC record available at https://lccn.loc.gov/2019055928

Distributed in Canada by Sterling Publishing Co., Inc.
c/o Canadian Manda Group, 664 Annette Street
Toronto, Ontario M6S 2C8, Canada
Distributed in the United Kingdom by GMC Distribution Services
Castle Place, 166 High Street, Lewes, East Sussex BN7 1XU, England
Distributed in Australia by NewSouth Books
University of New South Wales, Sydney, NSW 2052, Australia

For information about custom editions, special sales, and premium and corporate purchases, please contact Sterling Special Sales at 800-805-5489 or specialsales@sterlingpublishing.com.

Manufactured in the United States

Lot #:
2 4 6 8 10 9 7 5 3 1
11/21

sterlingpublishing.com

Hold fast to dreams
For if dreams die
Life is a broken-winged bird
That cannot fly.

~from *Dreams* by Langston Hughes

CHAPTER ONE

IF I ONLY HAD A BRAIN

Can you strut like the Scarecrow?
G-r-r-r like the Lion?
Or follow the Yellow Brick Road like Dorothy?
Then THE WIZ needs you!

Auditions after school Friday.
Ms. Hansberry's classroom.
Research *THE WIZ* and come prepared
with a one-minute monologue &
Stun us with sixteen bars of a show-stopping song.

It hadn't been two minutes since Ailey's last mini fiasco, but before Mr. Rock could even read the first word of the announcement, Ailey was out of his seat—again. He needed a closer look at the emerald green paper covered in silver script.

"I can definitely strut like the Scarecrow, Mr. R.," Ailey said. He popped his shoulders up and down, bouncing instep to a beat in his head.

Titters went through the class.

"Really, Mr. Lane?" Mr. Rock exhaled, crossing his arms. "How many recess points do you need to lose—today alone—to understand you need to stay parked in your chair like everyone else?"

Realizing defeat, Ailey bowed his head. Without a peep, he moonwalked down the row of desks, his feet sliding effortlessly across the linoleum like it was ice, before dropping back into his seat.

"There's more than just the Scarecrow in *The Wiz* anyway," Juano Hernandez, another student, said.

"Yeah," Mahalia Jackson, the know-it-all who didn't know-it-all, added, "There's also the all-powerful Wiz. My sister played her last year at summer camp. So, I already know all the lines."

Ailey grumbled. Mahalia *always* opened her mouth, and to make matters worse, Ailey had to look up at her a little, even while seated. Actually, he had to crane his neck to look up at most of his classmates, except for his best friend, Maceo Merriweather, the only kid shorter than he was in the whole fifth grade. "Who cares," he said when she turned his direction. "She can't beat the Scarecrow's moves." Ailey rocked his neck, hands up in a challenge.

4

"Dance won't get you anywhere," Mahalia said. "You need to know how to *act*."

Mr. Rock walked over and pressed his fingertips against Ailey and Mahalia's desks, his eyebrow lifted almost to his hairline. "I'm guessing you two don't want to take this party down to Principal Coppin's office? But that is exactly what is about to happen if I have to come over here again."

"But . . ." Mahalia whined then closed her mouth. But of course, she couldn't keep it that way as Ailey wormed his upper body toward her. "It's his fault. And I bet he doesn't even know what *The Wiz* is."

Ailey stopped. "Do too," he shot back, glaring at her. "Last year my parents took me and my sister to see it in New York. And the Scarecrow did his thing."

Mr. Rock tilted his head back toward the ceiling like Ailey's mother always did when she was "praying for strength." Then he looked between both of them. "We still have a few minutes before the bell. Why don't you enlighten those who may not know what it's all about?"

"Yeah, Miss Smarty-pants," Ailey baited. "What's *The Wiz* about?"

Mahalia laughed. "He's looking at you."

Ailey turned to see Mr. Rock staring him down, that eyebrow still talking to his hairline.

"Oh . . . um." Ailey straightened his polo shirt. "*The Wiz* is the Black version of *The Wizard of Oz*. The movie—

not the book we're reading. Some parts are way different from the book. But one thing's the same—the Scarecrow is the smartest of them all." He flapped his hand in the air, nodding along.

"Okay, Ailey. Thank you. That's enough, but he is right—"

"For once," Mahalia said, too low for Mr. Rock to hear, but Ailey did.

"The movie is a bit different from Baum's *The Wonderful Wizard of Oz*," continued Mr. Rock, addressing the whole class. "For one, in 1978 it was made with an all-Black cast, including people like Diana Ross, Michael Jackson, Lena Horne, and Richard Pryor. And now, thirty-two years later, in 2010, it will be made with all of you. I can't wait to see how you all make it your own. Plus, it'll be nice to see another one of the books we're reading come to life on our stage. So, I hope you'll all consider trying out."

Murmurs of excitement zipped through the class.

Mahalia tapped her finger against her lip, and her eyes roamed the room before landing on Ailey. "I think *I'm* going to be the Scarecrow," she informed the class, grinning at Ailey, as his mouth fell open. Her chubby cheeks looked crammed with gumballs. "I played Wilona in last year's production of *The Watsons Go to Birmingham*. I'm sure you all remember that standing ovation. Everyone said I was *amazing*."

"Whatever." Ailey squinched up his face. "I'd be a perfect Scarecrow with the skills I got." Ailey jumped up again and spun.

This time there were no titters from his class. They were too distracted, chattering about which roles they wanted.

"I'm glad you're excited," Mr. Rock said to him. "But the role isn't just about the dancing. You'd need to learn a number of lines as well. So, you may want to keep your options open. The stage crew is pretty cool. Maybe you'd want to consider something there?"

For once, Ailey's feet went still.

"Being out front is a huge responsibility," Mr. Rock went on. Though Ailey wished he wouldn't. "Lots of people would be counting on you."

"But I can do it," Ailey said. "Really." Suddenly he wasn't sure if he was trying to convince himself or Mr. Rock.

"Yeah, right," Mahalia snickered. "You'd mess that up too. Just like you messed up your poetry recital, your science presentation, and . . . oh, what else . . . *everything*."

"That's enough, Ms. Jackson." Mr. Rock clapped his hands once, silencing her and a couple students who dared giggle. "I'm never one to stand in someone's way," he said and turned back to Ailey. "So, if you think you're up for the Scarecrow, give auditions a try." He backed toward the front of the room. "I encourage you all to think about the best roles for each of you and go for them. And don't forget the

importance of the stage crew. They help make the magic happen. The play couldn't go on without them."

"But it definitely couldn't happen without the onstage talent," Mahalia cut in again.

"It takes everyone," Mr. Rock said returning to his desk.

"I can do it, Mr. R. You'll see." Ailey tried again, feeling a sting like a paper cut that instead of just being tiny, made your whole arm burn, taking over—EVERY. SINGLE. THOUGHT.

"Okay, Ailey," Mr. Rock sighed. "We'll see." He shuffled a stack of papers on his desk.

Another cut.

Ailey could tell his teacher wasn't convinced. But he would show him. He would show everyone, he could be the Scarecrow.

Then right on cue, the alarm on Ailey's Marvel Comic Black Panther watch growled, just as the dismissal bell rang. He snatched his bag off his seat and rushed toward the open door.

"Mr. Lane, *we* are walking, right? And class, don't forget to read chapter 16 of Baum's book tonight," Mr. Rock reminded. "And answer the questions at the end."

Everyone groaned.

But Ailey wasn't thinking about that now. All he wanted to do was get home to Grampa. He would believe Ailey could do it. This would be Ailey's big chance to show everyone he could be something besides a goof-off. Teachers weren't going to pass him over for important tasks anymore, and his sister, Jojo, wasn't going to be the only one in the family getting praised. It was his turn.

He was going to show everyone that he, Ailey Benjamin Lane, could be a star.

CHAPTER TWO

A LITTLE DIFFERENT FROM THE REST

I'm going to be the Scarecrow and it's going to be awesome," Ailey said, headed down the hall with his best friend, Maceo, who'd heard the announcement in his homeroom class.

"You sure you want the part?" Maceo asked.

"Why wouldn't I?" Ailey stopped, hoping his best friend didn't doubt him too.

"Mahalia, that's why. In homeroom, she kept going on and on about how she'll be the best Scarecrow anyone's ever seen." His eyes rolled up as he shook his head, his dreadlocks swinging. "I wouldn't want to do anything that involved competing against her. She probably bites worse than my neighbor's German Shepherd and he's a retired police dog. Plus, she has to win at *everything* or she gets in your face about it FOREVER," Maceo said. "I'm thinking of trying for the Lion. It'd be pretty cool to be fearless and all."

"I'm not scared of her."

"I am." Maceo wrinkled his nose, causing his glasses to tilt a little.

"I'm playing the Scarecrow and no one, especially not her, will stop me," Ailey said, pushing through the doors of the school.

"Okay . . ." Maceo shook his head again. "But don't say I didn't warn you."

Ailey glanced down at his Black Panther watch, a tenth birthday present he'd gotten two months before from Grampa. The clawed black hands of the Marvel comic character told him he was going to miss his window of opportunity to beat his sister home.

"You wanna come over and play Dungeon Avengers?" Maceo asked on the school's front stairs.

"I can't. I have to get home before Jojo. You know how she hogs the computer and I have some stuff to look up." Ailey barreled down the last steps. "Later," he called out to his friend.

"Later."

The April breeze tickled the leaves and nudged at the grass. Parents in parked cars, windows down, listened to talk radio or old people's music while waiting for their kids. Ailey sauntered down the tree-lined street, grinning and humming.

He threw out lines, trying to see which ones stuck.

I can flow like water
And shine like a star
I'm not too close
Yet I'm not too far
Actin' ain't nothin'
I got this y'all
Even with straw
Scarecrow's smart
Not dumb at all.
And although I notice how they doubt my skills
When I step on the stage I'm gonna show 'em the real.

Ailey slid, arms out, to one edge of the sidewalk. People gawked as he moonwalked over to the other side, holding his belt buckle. He bit his bottom lip and swayed his head. He felt like he was flying.

When he got to the corner of Fort Mose Avenue, he stopped across the street from the red brick building that was the center of his family's world. In the window of their hardware store, a dust rag hung from Grampa's hand. The display of paint cans and hanging brushes was spotless. Ailey was sure nothing even had a sprinkling of dust on it because Grampa had probably already cleaned the display more than once. He always said, *don't let the dust settle on nothin' you do. Stir it up. Don't let things be forgotten.*

Ailey rushed to the other sidewalk and shoved open the front door. A chime tingled over his head, alerting everyone a customer entered the store.

"It's just me," he called when his dad's head popped out from behind a shelf as he helped a customer.

"What up, Two Foot?" his dad said and then disappeared back behind the shelf.

Out of the corner of his eye, Ailey saw Grampa at the end of the cleaning aisle across from the window display. He was staring off, the rag still hung in his hand. A smile crinkled the skin at the corner of his eyes like he was in a trance. He hadn't even looked up when the entry bell rang out. He usually greeted customers three seconds before the bell chimed, every time.

Instead, this time, Grampa stared off, as if seeing something no one else could see. Although his upper body was almost completely still, his feet pivoted from toe to heel back to toe, as he tapped in place. His knees were slightly bent and his feet danced in a relaxed motion. Ailey paused for a second, staring. Grampa only tapped like that when he thought no one was watching.

"Pops. Hey, Pops," Ailey's dad called to Grampa. "Can you help Mr. Taylor pick a prybar and the right sealant?"

There was no answer from Grampa.

He still faced the window. And he still tapped.

"I apologize." Ailey heard his dad say. "My father-in-law's hearing isn't what it used to be. Let me go grab your replacement shingles, then I'll give you a hand out here."

Ailey went over and tugged on Grampa's sleeve. "Grampa, Grampa."

His feet stilled, as he blinked. Then he glanced down at Ailey as if just realizing where he was.

"Ah, there's my favorite skygazer," Grampa said. He pushed his newsboy cap back on his head a bit and pressed at his forehead with the back of his hand. His ears curled away from his head almost like an elf's. The same way Jojo's did. "You gonna be ready to give it a go tonight?"

"I'm not sure I can. I have important stuff to do first," Ailey said.

"Well, I hope you can. You know it isn't the same up there without my wingman. It's 'pose to be a clear night too. Not a cloud in the sky. But I understand. Not even the stars should come before homework."

"It's not homework, exactly." Ailey grinned.

Grampa reached for his wooden cane resting against the wall even though he always said it was more for show than need. "I see." He smiled. "Don't forget your Uncle Sammy's bringing his ole bones over here this weekend for Josephine's birthday, so we might not get another chance for a while."

"Ugh." Ailey's backpack hit the floor. Jojo's birthday was Saturday and he'd definitely tried to forget it. Even with her reminding everyone, even the mailman, every chance she got. "Something kind of important's come up though." A smile nearly split Ailey's face in two.

"Well now." Grampa's smile grew too. "Something more important than our skygazin'? Now you got me curious. Do tell. I've never known you to pass up an evening of trying to spot some stars."

"Grampa, I'm gonna be the Scarecrow in *The Wiz* and I need to practice!"

"The Scarecrow? That's a big part," Grampa said.

"The biggest." Ailey stretched out his arms. "He's a star."

"Alright then, you gonna be ready for such a big role?" Grampa studied Ailey's face.

Not Grampa too.

"I can do it." Ailey knocked his foot against his backpack not meeting Grampa's eyes.

"I *know* you can do it. That's not what I asked." Grampa rested his hand on Ailey's shoulder, raising his chin. "I asked if you're ready to put your mind to this. To get up on that stage."

Ailey smiled, relieved. "I got this, Grampa. You'll see. Everybody will."

"Okay, Jackrabbit. I hear you." Grampa lifted his hands, palms out. "Need any help with your lines?"

"No thanks. I'm really just going to dance. That's what everyone wants to see anyway." Ailey wobbled, moving his arms like he drove a car, then ran his hands past his head doing the Dougie.

Grampa slapped his thigh. "Alright now! We know you got moves. That's in your blood." Then his smile thinned out. "But I want to make sure you're learning the rest of the stuff you'll need. It ain't gonna be easy. Trust me, I know." He looked off in the distance. His hand rested over his cane.

"Grampa." The word hung in the air.

"Yeah, Jackrabbit?" Grampa shifted his gaze back to Ailey.

"How come you don't dance anymore? Gramma Franny always said you were great."

The corner of Grampa's lip turned up again. "I was somethin' in my day. But it's a long story, Jackrabbit. For another time," he sighed.

"That's what you *always* say."

"I know, I know. But I earned it—I'm old." He winked. "Besides, you don't need to hear about my old days of tappin'. Not when you have a role to prepare for, and I'm sure your mom and Josephine could help you too. And your dad—" He popped a spearmint candy in his mouth. "He's got some moves in him too now."

"No, I'm good." Ailey shook his head. "I told you, I got this. I kind of want to do it on my own."

"There's no shame in that. But just remember you got us if you need us."

"I know, Grampa."

"Don't let me hold you up." Grampa patted Ailey's shoulder. "You got a star to become."

Ailey couldn't hold back his smile as he Dougied the short distance to the register and the curtain that divided the front of the store from the storage area and the back office. He nodded his head pretending to slick his hair to an imagined beat, rocking his knees low as he did a shimmy-strut, almost colliding with his dad when he emerged from the back holding a box of shingles and a pair of pliers.

"*Whoa*. My bad, Dad. My fault." Ailey continued his wobble-rock around him. "I've got work to do."

His dad swung his arm up, balancing the box over Ailey's head. His muscles flexed. "What's that move, Two Foot?"

"It's the Dougie."

"The *Dougie?*"

"Yeah, it's new, it just came out."

His dad popped and locked his arms out straight, then he bent one up and the other down like a robot. "Well in that case: *You need to Dougie upstairs/there's no time to waste.*"

"Come on, Dad. Can you sound any cornier?" Ailey smacked his hand against his forehead.

"Okay, okay." His dad nodded, pointing a finger at Ailey. Then he held the pliers out toward Ailey like a microphone. "Show me how it's done then."

"*Time is a ticking clock . . .*" Ailey said, searching the ceiling for the next words. But his dad jumped in.

"*Always going and never stops,*" he finished for him. "*The only direction is to the top.*" A smile pressed to his lips. "*Just make sure it's a swish when you take your shot.*"

"*Awww,* sweet!" Ailey grinned.

"*I just showed you how it's done, so give me my props.*" His dad extended his hand, waiting for a fist bump.

Ailey laughed. "Okay, Dad." He pushed his fist against his dad's. His smile wider than wide. He wanted to keep rhyming, but his dad still had a customer and Jojo would be home any minute.

Ailey was up the back stairs and in his family's apartment above the store before anyone could have said "Scarecrow" three times fast.

He dropped his bag in the middle of the hallway and kicked off his sneakers, nearly tripping over Grampa's one-eyed, farting bulldog that left a pool of slobber in his wake. "Sorry, King!"

Ailey dashed across the living room to the computer. He'd beat Jojo, who always claimed she had homework to do, even though she was always on video chats or looking up stupid bedazzle projects, clicking off the screens and back to her assignments when anyone walked in the room. He slid onto the seat at the desk and rubbed his hands together like he was about to dig into his favorite meal of crab legs.

"Oh, no you don't, mister," his mom called from the doorway.

"But I have research to do!" Ailey clamped his feet around the legs of the chair, keeping his bottom firmly planted on the cushion.

"*Um hmmm?*" Mom crossed her arms at her chest and stared, not quite believing him. Her Ailey Lie Detector, or A.L.D as Ailey joked, was in full power mode, searching Ailey's face. "Don't get me wrong, I'm thrilled you're trying to get a head start on your *work*, but not before you pick up this bag, move your shoes, and give your mother a kiss."

Without grumbling, he rose from the chair, pecked her cheek, lined up his shoes, tossed his bag into the basket next to Jojo's violin case, and was back at the computer before she took a full breath.

"What's the rush?" she asked.

"Ummm . . . it's a surprise," he said.

"Really now?" She narrowed her eyes, searching his face. "It better not have me coming down to that school again."

"It won't, I promise." Ailey swung back around to the computer. "Well, at least not to Principal Coppin's office. You'll come see me on the stage . . ." *Oops.*

19

"The stage?" She stepped closer. "And what exactly will you be doing up there?"

There goes the surprise.

"I'll be *acting*."

"Acting?" Her brows nearly touched, then relaxed.

"Yep, you'll see. I'm going to be great."

"I don't doubt you could be," she said. "Just be ready to work."

"I will." Some of Ailey's excitement seeped out like a deflating balloon. *Did she doubt him too?*

Then she grinned as if knowing his thoughts. "Don't get your feathers all ruffled. I just want you to practice and really try. Like I always tell Jojo before her violin recitals, you don't have to be perfect. You just have to give it your best. I'll be cheering for you." She spread her warm hands across his cheeks and tilted his head up. "I always do, you know?" She kissed his nose and then left him to his work.

He turned back to the computer, shaking the mouse 'til the screen lit up with a family photo in front of the Black American West Museum. He quickly typed in THE WIZ and hit: enter. Songs, videos lyrics, and parts of the original script filled the screen.

He pressed print on almost all of it, and then he downloaded the videos to his Nano so he could watch and listen to them later because he knew Jojo would never let him have the computer all night. Neither would his mom. Then he typed in THE WIZ THE SCARECROW. Images of the Scarecrow with a painted dot for a nose in a fuzzy white and orange striped sweater bombarded the screen.

Almost every image was the same. The same striped sleeves, a dumpy garbage-looking shirt, floppy brown pants, and a funny paper lunch bag hat. Ailey scrolled through the pictures. Even the ones that weren't from the original movie looked the same. Everyone made the Scarecrow's outfit look lame, wack, or just plain boring, when he was the coolest in the show.

"He might have the flyiest moves, but those clothes . . ." Ailey mumbled, shaking his head.

Then he had an idea—he always had an idea!

He'd be a special kind of Scarecrow. Different than all the rest.

"Grampa always says, in order to stand out, think outside of what's expected," Ailey said to the screen.

He wouldn't just be *another* Scarecrow at the auditions, he'd be a different kind of Scarecrow. With the best dance moves anyone had ever seen. He inched his hands up, slow, swaying and flexing.

He was going to get everyone's attention.

CHAPTER THREE

TRYOUTS VS. THE BLACK HOLE

I t looked like every kid in the school had turned up for tryouts.

The audition line snaked all the way from Ms. Hansberry's door down the hall to the principal's office, a place Ailey knew all too well.

Some of Ailey's schoolmates wore aluminum foil hats, whiskers, paw mittens, and tails. A number of girls had bedazzled silver or apple red shoes.

Ailey smirked, his head high. Thick-framed black glasses rested on his nose. Nobody looked as fine as he did striding down the hall, decked out from head to toe in style. The orange, blue, and brown plaid suit he'd worn to Auntie Simone's swearing-in as a judge, fit him just right. His brown tweed vest, gingham shirt, and tangerine tie were saying something, as Grampa always said. And Ailey knew that what they were saying was good. He wasn't just another scarecrow. His socks were even a cool orange and brown geometric pattern. His brown shoes shined. When he glanced down, he could just make out his faint reflection. He winked. "He-ll-oooo, Handsome."

He pulled at the sides of the Kangol hat he'd worn a couple Halloweens before, when he, Jojo, and Dad had dressed like Run DMC. He even exaggerated his stride, matching the Crow's Anthem playing on repeat in his earbuds, so his gold rope chain would swing.

He knew he looked fly.

And just so no one would forget he was supposed to be filled with newspaper and hay, he had a couple pieces of newspaper peeking from under his hat and tucked in his breast pocket and up his sleeves.

Almost everyone turned his way, either smiling or squealing to another classmate. A couple of the guys strutted in place, copying Ailey.

When he reached the end of the audition line, there was Mahalia. She wore a little straw hat cocked to the side. Her curls were sprayed golden and bright yellow strings stuck out of her hair like strands of straw.

"Attention, everyone," Ms. Hansberry called down the line.

As always, her shoes were one of the colors out of a Skittles bag. Today, they were sour apple green.

Ailey liked her style.

He smoothed out the front of his suit, ready to impress.

"I'm thrilled you're all trying out for this year's production." She placed her hand over her heart. "In the interest of time, we're splitting everyone into groups. Dorothys meet at the water fountain. The Scarecrows—"

"That's me." Ailey bolted around his classmates and sprang out of line.

"Stop bussin'," Mahalia hissed. She elbowed him. Even for a girl, she was as strong and as tall as any Pee-Wee football linebacker. "I was before you."

Ailey winced and rubbed his side.

"I don't even know why you're here," Mahalia said. "I'm going to get the role. I already see my name in that program." She loomed over him, tapping the air with her finger for each word she said. "The Scarecrow played by the wonderfully talented and beautiful Mahalia Jackson."

"That'd be a typo. You know you're the Wicked Witch." While she sucked her teeth, thinking of a comeback, Ailey slipped by her.

"Scarecrows, you're up," Ms. Hansberry said at the same time. She held a clipboard with a pen dangling from it on a polka-dot ribbon. "After you sign in, please go into the music room and have a seat."

She handed it to the students at the front of the line. Right before she got to Ailey, he pushed up his chin, standing as tall as he could.

"Well now," she said scanning his outfit. "Interesting choice of costume. I wouldn't have thought of it. A distinguished hip-hop Scarecrow . . . I like it."

His cheeks pressed back into the biggest smile he thought he had ever made.

She held out the clipboard and he signed it before Mahalia could grab the pen. Then he passed it back. "Make sure you keep this paper, Ms. H. It's going to be worth money someday."

"I'll keep that in mind." Her eyes twinkled as she pointed toward the door, which Ailey sauntered through.

☆ ☆ ☆

By the fifth monologue, Ailey was finding it hard to keep himself awake. The students before him all read their lines as-stiff-as-tin-men or whispered like cowardly lions.

Ailey knew he'd be better. He'd stayed up every night practicing and had the *Crow's Anthem* on loop in his Nano, plus he had a secret weapon: he could dance. For the whole week, whenever he could get on the computer before Jojo, he watched music videos to learn all the dance moves he could. If it was a cool move since he was born, he tried it. And got pretty good at a lot of them.

Out of habit, he reached down to fiddle with his Black Panther watchband, but it wasn't there. His stomach dropped—he'd forgotten the good luck charm Grampa had given him. *How hadn't he noticed before?*

"You're next, Ailey," Ms. Hansberry said. "Come on up here and wow us."

He pushed the thought of his lucky watch to the back of his mind and sprang to his feet. "Don't mind if I do."

When he got to the piano, he stretched like a track star readying for a race.

"Are you starting with the monologue or the song?" Ms. Hansberry played a few chords on the piano.

"I'm starting with some fire." Ailey lifted his leg, twisting his foot in the air.

"That's great, but in the interest of time, can you boogie and sing, or shimmy and recite?" Ms. Hansberry played a sort of drum roll on the piano.

"I, um, thought I'd just do the dancing first," Ailey said. "Then you won't need to hear anything else."

"Hmmm. We need to see a little more than just the dancing I'm afraid. Sprinkle a bit of the monologue in there too." She moved her hands across the air like she still played piano keys.

"Okay, but I think my moves are what the crowd will really want to see." Ailey tried to protest. He hadn't really tried to learn the lines. He didn't think he'd need to.

"I hear you, but I'm sorry, we don't have much time."

Ms. Hansberry nodded toward the clock. "We have other Scarecrows after you, and I still need to get to the lions, tin men, and Totos."

Ailey cleared his throat. *What was that first line? Come on, come on, THINK!*

His hand reached for his bare wrist again. And his heart tripled its beat.

The room went quiet. All eyes were on him.

He blinked, trying to ignore a strange feeling creeping close. As he stared at his classmates and they stared at him, waiting, his mind went blank, like someone hit erase. Something wasn't right. He didn't like having all those eyes on him. He stood stock still trying to remember anything. A word. A lyric. A beat. A move.

Nothing.

"Ms. Hansberry," Mahalia whined, "He doesn't even know any lines. Can I have my turn now?"

"That's enough, Mahalia." Ms. Hansberry cut her a look then refocused on Ailey. "You ready?"

"I—I—I," Ailey stammered. His schoolmates kept staring. He wished they'd stop. He couldn't think with them all watching him. Ready to laugh. Waiting to see him fail. His thumb kept rubbing his skin where his watch should've been. So many words filled his head: *You? Maybe next time. No. Don't try. Maybe try something else . . .* But none of them were the words he needed. The words to the monologue or the lyrics to a song. Mahalia slid back in her chair and huffed, crossing her arms.

"Do you want to give someone else a chance and try again in a couple minutes?" Ms. Hansberry encouraged. Her lips pulled thin in that strained way people smiled when they felt really, really bad for you. Ailey knew that look—well.

He had to do something before he disappointed the last teacher who still had faith in him.

He turned to Ms. Hansberry. "I'm just going to dance first."

"Okay, then, Ailey." She sounded doubtful but didn't stop him this time.

He got in his opening stance and rocked. Everyone's eyes were still on him. *Wait . . . what was the next step?*

Heat crept up his back, under his collar, and spread to his shoulders. Students fidgeted in their chairs, cupped hands over mouths, whispered, snickered, and smirked.

It was hopeless.

He knew nothing: not the words, not the song, not even the moves. Ailey's memory had been sucked into a black hole. He couldn't even remember *any* of his favorite dances, like he'd forgotten how to catch a beat. Even his pitiful attempt at the Dougie went sideways. The newspaper in his pocket, his Kangol, oversize Run DMC glasses, and fake gold chain suddenly felt ridiculous.

"Ms. Hansberry, can I go now?" Mahalia interrupted again. "You won't need to see anyone else after you see me anyway."

"I said that's enough, Mahalia. We can spare a couple more seconds." Ms. Hansberry floated around the piano toward Ailey. "Would you like to give it one more shot?"

Ailey didn't raise his eyes to look at her. He'd failed her too. "No. I'm done."

His chin dropped even lower and he took off the glasses as he slunk past giggling schoolmates. He wished he could get swallowed in the same black hole that had sucked out his memory and his moves.

"Listen everyone, don't worry if you stumble," Ms. Hansberry said in her gentlest voice. "There will be other opportunities to be involved, and there will *always* be other plays. And for those of you who make Monday's callbacks, be ready to wow us some more."

Ailey felt her watching him, but he didn't raise his head.

"It's my turn." Mahalia popped out of her seat, her hand in the air.

She brushed past Ailey. "Step aside, scaredy pants. Watch. And. Learn."

"I wasn't scared," Ailey grumbled.

"Well, you sure weren't good," Mahalia threw back over her shoulder. "But now you'll see great. F sharp, please, Ms. Hansberry." Mahalia handed over her sheet music when she reached the piano.

Ailey sucked his teeth, peeling off the Kangol, newspaper strips falling as Mahalia's booming voice filled the room. From the very first note, everyone took notice. She sounded as good as the singers on the radio. Everyone said she could sing, but he had no clue she could SING. He'd skipped last year's performance of *The Watsons Go to Birmingham*. Then, as if he didn't feel bad enough, she held her last note longer than Ailey could hold his breath underwater. When she finished, everyone whistled and clapped. Ailey shoved his hands in his pockets.

Round One went to Mahalia.

CHAPTER FOUR

WISHES NEED WARNING LABELS TOO

When Ailey pushed through the school doors, he wasn't ready to face the questions at home. He wanted to lock himself in his room forever.

"Hey, Ailey. Wait up," Maceo shouted behind him. His backpack hung low, crammed with almost every book in the world, weighing him down as he ran. "How'd it go?" Maceo had smudged the lion whiskers that stretched across his face in black paint, but you couldn't tell unless you were close.

"I don't want to talk about it," Ailey grumbled.

"How come?" Maceo pressed.

"*I'll* tell you how come." Dewey, one of their classmates interrupted.

He strode toward them laughing, hands hugging his belly like he'd just heard the world's funniest joke.

"Hey, Lane, look familiar?" Dewey asked.

He stood at the edge of the grass nibbling at his fingers

like they were corn on the cob and wiggling his legs like he was trying to shake a bug free from inside his pants. Then he let his body free fall.

"Splat!" he yelled as he hit the ground, his arms and legs spread in funny angles like a cartoon character that'd run straight out of a ten-story window and crashed.

"Nice one," Ailey snorted, walking away as kids around him cracked up.

Grampa always said, *don't let nobody see the sweat 'round your collar.*

Maceo just looked confused. It was obvious he was one of the only people in the whole school who hadn't heard about Ailey's massive fail.

"What was that?" he asked as they turned down the block away from the school and the laughter.

"Nothing," Ailey said. His fingers dug into the strap of his book bag. "See ya."

"Thought you were coming over?" Maceo stopped, watching him.

"*Naw*, not today," Ailey mumbled.

All Ailey wanted to do was crawl deep under his covers and hide. He knew Grampa and his mom would have a gazillion questions about tryouts and he didn't want to answer any of them. They probably wouldn't even be surprised he failed. And since Uncle Sammy was coming for

Jojo's birthday and always slept in his room, Ailey wanted a couple hours of alone time before all the real questions began. Grampa's older brother didn't cut corners with his words, *he told straight truth*, like Grampa always said. Right then though, Ailey wasn't sure he was ready to hear all Uncle Sammy's true opinions.

Ailey skulked around the block to the entrance of the hardware store and peered in the window. No one was in sight. Instead of shoving open the door like he usually did, he pushed it slowly and squeezed inside so the bell wouldn't ring and snuck down a side aisle. He came to a halt at the curtain to the back office. His dad stood at the side door signing for a delivery. Ailey dashed by, crept up the stairs, dropped his bag inside the apartment, kicked off his shoes, and headed to his room.

Now all he wanted was to bury his head in his pillow and get lost in his Dungeon Avengers video game all weekend with no questions about tryouts, the Scarecrow, or his dance moves.

He peeled off his outfit, feeling like an imposter. He didn't have what it took to be a Scarecrow different from the rest unless that meant being one who failed. So many things had gone wrong. For starters, he had forgotten to wear his lucky Black Panther watch. He snatched it off the side table. "Where were you when I needed you?" he said staring at the crouched Marvel character on his watch face. He pushed a button on the side of it and a beam of light shot across the room. A hologram of the Black Panther spread across his wall. Another button produced his alarm's low growl. Even though the instruction manual warned against pointing the beam directly at someone because it might cause temporary blindness, Ailey wished he'd had it at tryouts for the audience, to make it so bright, people couldn't see his massive fail.

Ailey flopped back on his bed; he didn't want to think about auditions, but it filled every inch of his brain. He couldn't believe how wrong it had all gone for him and how perfect it'd been for Mahalia.

"All of it was stupid," he grumbled, twisting to his side. "Who cares about being a scarecrow, anyway?" he said to the Black Panther hologram that shook on the wall as he moved his arm.

He did. That's who.

Ailey curled in a ball trying to forget. Then his door creaked open. He pushed the button on his watch. The Black Panther vanished.

He pretended to sleep until King's cold, wet nose touched his hand. He relaxed and rolled over and petted the slobbering dog on the head.

"I really messed up today," he said honestly. King wouldn't tell anyone.

King watched him and of course said nothing, but Ailey

could tell he understood; he always did. Smelling no treats, he plopped down on Ailey's floor and started snoring. Even though he didn't want them to come, Ailey glanced at his half-open door wondering why Mom or Grampa hadn't already poked their heads in to ask how everything went. *They already knew I wouldn't be good enough*, he thought.

He always messed up.

He turned away from the door, pressing his cheek into his pillowcase, and started mumbling a rap to the rhythm of King's snores.

> *I always seem to screw up like this*
> *Crash like this*
> *Burn like this*
> *Maybe I'm not meant for a spotlight to shine like this*
> *My talent might be duckin' and divin' and always*
>   *goofin' off.*
> *But when I froze up like ice*
> *I just wish I could've dissolved.*

"Ailey, wake up, son. Wake up."

"Dad?" Ailey turned looking around his room. The late afternoon light dimmed behind his curtains. "What time is it?"

"Almost five." His dad's voice was low. "I need you to get up."

"Why? It's Friday, can't I sleep a little bit and do chores later?"

"This isn't about your chores or your homework. Grampa Benji's in the hospital."

"Grampa?" Ailey sprung out of bed. "Is he okay? What happened?"

"We'll know more when we get there. They just finished running tests, but your mom says he got dizzy and took a nasty fall. She's there with your sister. I'm going to grab a couple of his things to make him more comfortable."

Ailey was changed and downstairs faster than a rocket could leave the earth's atmosphere.

"You ready?" His dad met him at the bottom of the stairs with a small duffle bag and the framed picture of Gramma Franny that sat next to Grampa's bed. It was the last thing Grampa saw when he went to sleep and the first when he woke. He always said his day wouldn't be right if he couldn't say good morning and good night to his favorite girl.

"Is he going to be okay?" Ailey asked.

"Not sure. We'll just have to wait and see." His dad turned off the lights and shut the door behind them.

Ailey suddenly felt guilty. All that time he'd been so relieved no one had bothered him. And all that time it hadn't been because they didn't believe in him, but because something had happened to Grampa.

CHAPTER FIVE

WORDS CAN BE KRYPTONITE

Ailey had wanted to be left alone, but not like this. Not with Grampa in the hospital.

When Ailey got to room 264, he didn't waste a breath. He ran to the side of the bed and threw himself against Grampa.

"*Ughf,*" Grampa sighed.

"Careful," Ailey's mom said from a chair near the bed. Jojo sat on a narrow bench on the other side. Her fingers raced across her lit phone screen tapping out a message while the faint beat of a song escaped through earbuds wedged in her ears. Their eyes met, hers were glassy. She quickly dropped her gaze and swatted her fingers at her cheek.

"Grampa, are you okay?" Ailey said, turning back to Grampa. "What happened?"

Grampa patted the side of Ailey's face and smiled, but Ailey could see he was in a bit of discomfort, probably from

Ailey pressing against his chest. Ailey loosened his grip. Grampa groaned quietly but his smile never fell.

"How was school today?" he asked. "How were auditions?" He spoke like it was any ordinary day, as if he weren't lying in a hospital, tubes snaking out of his arms and chest.

"Grampa, who cares about that?"

"I do," Grampa said. "How'd it go? You being the Scarecrow and all."

Ailey couldn't find the words to tell Grampa he'd failed.

"Yeah, how did it go, sweetie?" his mom asked, pulling Ailey's hand toward her. She sounded tired. She'd been sitting and worrying over Grampa for a while, waiting for the tests and for Ailey and Dad to arrive, while they sat in endless traffic.

"I heard it didn't go so well." Jojo looked up again, pulling her earbuds from her ears. "He got scared."

"I didn't get scared." Ailey balled his hands up. *Why did everyone keep saying that?*

Jojo shrugged. "That's what I heard."

Ailey cut his eyes at her. He wished she'd go back to her music. "What do you know? You don't even go to Hammon. I just forgot stuff that's all. I'll remember next time."

"Next time? There's gonna be one?" Jojo looked down at her phone when it flashed, then glanced back at Ailey. "Marisol, who *does* go to Hammon, told her sister, Marievette, who told Keke, who told me that her little cousin, Mahalia *killed* it as usual. And that she's the Scarecrow."

Ailey shook his head wishing he could shove her blinged-out phone in her mouth to shut her up. "That's not true. Ms. Hansberry hasn't decided yet. They still have callbacks."

"Your phone won't be ringing."

"That's enough, Josephine," their mom cut in. "I'm sure he tried his best. Didn't you?" She still held Ailey's hand and gave it a gentle squeeze so he would turn to her. He didn't.

"Mom, is it okay if we don't talk about it? It's over anyway," Ailey said.

"Fine, sweetie, fine." Her eyes were puffy behind her turquoise frames.

Ailey wanted to crawl through the floor again. Adding failure and disappointment to everything going wrong just then was the last thing he wanted to do.

"Pops, I brought you a few things to make you more comfortable," Ailey's dad said, filling the silence. He walked over to Grampa and slid the overnight bag on the cart at the foot of the bed.

"Appreciate it, son."

The warmth of Mom's hand slipped from Ailey's as she unfolded Gramma Franny's old throw quilt to lay it across Grampa's hospital bed.

Every part of Grampa's face lifted and then brightened

even more when Dad handed him the photo of Gramma Franny.

"*Ahh*, you didn't forget my girl," he said to Dad. "We never forget our girls, do we?" He winked at Dad, then glanced over at Mom, who pressed her cheek into Dad's shoulder as he wrapped his arm around her like she was cold.

"You need anything else, Daddy?" Mom asked. Ailey fiddled with his watchband at the side of the bed.

"Mind giving us a sec?" Grampa nodded toward Ailey.

Mom was about to protest, but Dad spoke to her in their secret language that only passed between their eyes. "I guess it's not a bad idea to go find some food," she said, giving in.

Dad nodded.

Mom rounded the corner of the bed and kissed Grampa. Then she patted Jojo's knee.

Jojo's eyebrows pushed together as she pulled out her earbuds. "We're leaving?"

"No, just getting a bite to eat. It's been a long day. And your Dad is going to get Uncle Sammy. You want to keep him company, get out of here for a little while?" She glided her hand down a few of Jojo's braids. Then she turned back to Grampa and Ailey. "We'll be back soon."

"We'll be fine," Grampa said as they left.

"He's not coming too?" Jojo asked, annoyed, watching

Ailey hover by Grampa's bed as their dad slung his arm over her shoulder leading her out the door.

"He's keeping him company while we take care of everything else."

From her expression, Ailey could tell she didn't like that idea. He understood. He just wanted to be with Grampa too.

"When are you coming home?" Ailey blurted out when they were gone.

"I'm not so sure, Jackrabbit. I'm not too certain it's in the plans for me this time around."

"What do you mean? You seem okay to me. You probably just need a little more rest, but you can get that at home. I can make sure you have everything you need."

"Maybe," Grampa said.

But that *maybe* sounded a lot like no.

"So, tell me about that audition. What happened?"

"Nothing happened." Ailey glanced away. "I don't want to talk about that now."

"Come on, Jackrabbit. We're cut from the same cloth, you and me. I know when something's troubling you, just as sure as when something's troubling me."

Ailey slumped; he never kept anything from Grampa. "I froze. I couldn't remember a thing."

"Well, that happens to the best of us sometimes. But that

doesn't mean you give up," Grampa said, pausing. "You're *not* givin' up, are you?"

Ailey bit at the inside of his cheek. "It's not up to me anymore. Besides Mahalia was awesome."

"That the girl sweet on you?"

"*Eeww*, Grampa."

"*Eeww*, nothing. I knew I loved your Gramma when I was just about your age. From the first second I saw her getting out of her daddy's shiny black Buick, in a pretty yellow dress with a sparkling white collar, I was seeing stars. Her smile could give me breath for a thousand years." He glanced over at the picture of Gramma Franny in the silver frame dad had brought. A big fabric flower tucked in her hair.

"Trust me, Grampa, you'll never hear me saying that about Mahalia." Ailey gagged. "I'm just saying she was better at being the Scarecrow, that's all." Ailey shoved his hands in his jacket pockets. "I'm never trying out for anything again."

"Eh, what I tell you about that word *never*?" Grampa lifted his index finger in warning.

"*Never* is a word I should *never* use," Ailey said like a chant, "Because it limits my possibilities."

"Exactly." Grampa kept poking at the air. "Show your strength. Do what you're good at. That's what my Nanna Truth always use to say."

"But after watching Mahalia, I'm not sure I'm good at *anything*."

"Hush now, I don't want to hear such talk. Find a way to trick yourself out of being scared. And try."

"I'm not scared."

Grampa cocked his head to the side. He had an Ailey Lie Detector of his own.

"I wasn't at first," Ailey argued. Then, sliding one hand from his pocket, he pulled at a loose thread on Gramma Franny's old quilt. "But it all went wrong. Everyone kept staring at me and I forgot it all."

Grampa leaned forward. "Sounds like you were acting more like that cowardly lion than a scarecrow with a brain."

"Maybe," Ailey admitted. "But not everyone's as brave as you, Grampa. And I even forgot my lucky watch." He lifted his arm.

"You don't need that. Your strength doesn't come from it or anyone else but you." He tapped Ailey's chest like it was a bull's-eye. "I gave you that watch 'cause it's nifty, not because it's lucky."

"Well, it couldn't have hurt if I'd had it," Ailey muttered.

Grampa stared at him long and hard. Then he squinted, nodding, as if deciding something. A far-off look in his eyes like when he tapped.

"Listen here, Jackrabbit," he said a moment later turning toward the window. "I've a secret to tell you."

CHAPTER SIX

DO SECRETS LIVE IN BOXES?

"A secret?" Ailey moved like a fly to a flytrap—*zzzzip*. Grampa had his attention. "What kind of secret?"

"We'll get to that. Rest yourself," Grampa said.

Like Ailey could do any such thing. It was like Grampa had waved tickets to Wakanda in his face and then snatched them back! Now all Ailey could think about was the secret and what it might be. But he also knew Grampa. No matter how much he begged or pushed, Grampa wouldn't be rushed.

Sometimes Ailey thought Grampa made him wait as a class in patience. And no one who knew Ailey would say he was getting an A+ in that.

"Is the sky clear out there tonight?" Grampa asked, as if he had all night to count the stars. Like nothing else was more important.

Ailey trudged over to the window and pulled up the blinds. "Yeah, it's pretty clear." He stared out into the night, hoping Grampa would talk.

"Turn out the lights so we can see real good. We always do our best thinking and talking when we're looking up at the stars."

When Ailey switched off the lights, buttons on the machines around Grampa glowed and flashed in the dark. He looked back outside, trying to tune out the beeps and hisses. He wanted to forget where they were. *Why they were there*. He wanted them to be up on the roof like they had planned to be.

"You got the Drinking Gourd yet?" Grampa asked.

"I think so." It had taken Ailey a few extra minutes to get his bearings in the night sky. He had looked up at the stars so many times with Grampa, but this wasn't their roof, and the lights around the hospital made it a little hard to see. Though Grampa's window faced the pitch-black woods. Ailey slid his finger across the glass, tracing the stars that formed the Big Dipper. It was the gathering of stars they always found first. And as always, Grampa started singing low and deep.

> *When the sun come back,*
> *and the firs' quail calls,*
> *Then the time is come.*
> *Follow the drinkin' gourd.*

Ailey said nothing as Grampa sang. He just peered out

at the night, pretending they were on the roof, waiting for Grampa's questions and his history lesson, because they always came.

"You know the reason it's called the Drinking Gourd, don't cha?"

"Yeeessss, sir," Ailey couldn't help but smile when he turned. *At least this part hadn't changed.*

"Well," Grampa said, cupping his hand over his ear, causing it to poke out even more. "Speak up, son. What is it?"

"People in Africa thought the Big Dipper looked like the shell of a dried fruit they used for making bowls and big spoons and stuff. And enslaved people in America thought so too. So they called it the Drinking Gourd."

"That's right. And the enslaved followed that gathering of stars and the North Star to what they desired most: freedom." He let out a raspy breath and Ailey stiffened. Grampa took a drink of water. When he raised a finger again and spoke, his voice was strong. "Know your history, Jackrabbit, so you can know yourself!"

Ailey relaxed at the familiar words. "Yes, sir." But he was ready to hear Grampa's secret.

Grampa almost always made the same speech whenever they studied the sky. But this time, Ailey couldn't help but think the Yellow Brick Road he was reading about in class was a lot like the Drinking Gourd. For the Scarecrow, the

Tin Man, the Lion, and Dorothy, it helped lead them to what they each wanted most: brains, a heart, courage, and home.

Ailey's finger traced the Drinking Gourd's bowl up to the Little Dipper and the North Star, which shined bright in the Little Dipper's handle.

"My eyes aren't what they use to be," Grampa said squinting. "But we can always see the North Star, the guiding star of sea captains, enslaved runaways, and any soul that's searching. Like my dad always told me, if you're ever lost, find Polaris, the Guiding Star. No matter where you are, it will be there. That's the beauty of stars. The same ones I see here, I could see as a boy in Harlem." Then he got lost in the sky for a while. Neither of them said a word.

It took all Ailey's will not to ask about the secret. Then he heard Grampa whisper. "All is well, Aida. All is well."

"Grampa, who's Aida?" Ailey asked instead, sensing Grampa wasn't ready to share his secret.

"Look back out that window," Grampa said. "And tell me if you see a little shimmering star just under Venus?"

Ailey turned back toward the window. But he couldn't see it.

"That sparkling, little star, I call Aida's Star."

Ailey kept studying the sky, searching for the large, silvery disk-like light that was Venus. "How come?" he asked.

"After my baby sister."

Ailey whipped his head around. "What? You have a sister? How come I didn't know that?"

"She died when I was a bit younger than you." Grampa took another heavy breath and nestled back against his pillows. "But she is the reason I skygaze. When I was about seven, we moved from Louisiana and Aida didn't take well to the North. I used to bundle her up and bring her out on the fire escape to get some night air. At first, I didn't want to, but momma insisted, and like your mom, when Momma Zelda said something, you listened."

And when Grampa told stories, Ailey listened. He loved to hear Grampa talk about their family. He walked over to Grampa's hospital bed and leaned in close. *Almost* forgetting about the secret.

"We would sit out there, bored. Me rockin' her and her crying. So, one day I started tappin' with her boppin' in my arms and she giggled. It was the best sound you could've ever heard. Made me feel like a superhero, like your Black Panther, me being the one to get it out of her." He nodded toward the sky, his smile broad. "Once she was right and happy, I settled us down and pointed to the twinkling stars. Her little head moved, following my finger 'til her eyelids slipped closed. I started looking forward to our time out there. But when she was about to turn two, she got real sick and never did come back from it.

"The night she left us, I climbed out on the fire

escape—our spot—wailin' like a baby myself. To be closer to her. I was the only one who could stop her cryin', so I was trying to stop my own. And you know what?" He glanced at Ailey, then looked back to the window. "That little star by Venus started shinin' and twinkling that night like I had never seen before. I knew it was Aida. Letting me know she was safe and outta pain."

"Really?" Ailey looked over his shoulder back toward the glass, his elbows pressed into the quilt.

"I swear to you." Grampa held up one palm and placed the other over his heart. "When I saw that star shining bright on me, I started tappin' to it. And I even sang. I mean singing ain't really my thing, but that night I did a whole bunch of singing and talking and dancing for that star. And in my heart of hearts, with every twinkle, Aida was giggling. I never did tell nobody about my star. But whenever I saw it shining and twinkling, I used to tell it all my secrets and dreams. I grew up telling that star my stories." Grampa looked away from the window back at Ailey. "I know it sounds foolish, but I sure did believe it was her, and truth be told, I still do." He grinned, settling his head back. "And you can tell it your stories and secrets too."

"I don't need to," Ailey said. "I have you. You're the one I tell everything to."

"But there will come a day when I won't be right here, but I'll still want to listen."

Ailey's brow crinkled and he tilted his head. "Don't say that."

"I have to, Jackrabbit. I want you to always know you can look out in the night sky and find me."

"But you aren't going anywhere, Grampa. You're gonna come home. You're fine." Ailey pressed his head into Grampa's lap.

"Everything okay in here?" Ailey's mom poked her head inside the doorway. "Why are the lights off?"

"We're fine," Grampa said. "Just skygazin'."

"Alright then," she said. "I'll leave you to it a little longer, but, Ailey, you need to eat and Dad needs to rest." She closed the door and Ailey heard her heels click across the floor in the hall.

After a few minutes Grampa patted the quilt next to him. "Stop your fretting and come sit up here with me for a second. I want to tell you something."

Ailey climbed up and sniffled. He wiped the back of his hand over his eyes.

"There is no need for tears," Grampa said. "I've had a good long life. Filled with so much. So if the good Lord is ready for me to come home, who am I to complain? Your Gramma Franny been up there long enough without me."

"But what about me? Mom? Jojo and Dad? You can't leave us." Ailey knew he sounded selfish and whiny, but he didn't care.

"It might not be up to me, but I want you to listen real good and promise me you won't ever give up on what you truly want. Not even when it's hard." Grampa leaned back, looking Ailey in the eyes. "Don't let regret, lost dreams, and missed opportunities carry you down like they did me."

"What do you mean?"

Grampa stared off again.

"Regrets stay with you forever. They're feisty. They won't let you shake 'em, no matter how much you try."

Ailey knotted his finger in the cuff of his pants. He'd never heard Grampa talk like this or look so serious. Then Grampa focused again, and his eyes met Ailey's as if he knew he was beginning to worry him. His gaze softened and his shoulders relaxed. The tight lines around his mouth slipped away. "I need you to promise me something else too."

"Yes, sir."

"Promise me you'll help me with my secret."

"I will, Grampa. I'm ready." Whatever Grampa was about to tell him, Ailey was determined not to let him down.

Grampa nodded. "I think it's 'bout time I let it go." He stared at Ailey for a long moment. "Now listen here, when I'm gone, I need you to do this for me—"

"Stop, Grampa."

"Hush now." Grampa covered Ailey's hand with his own. His fingers were the same brown as Ailey's, only more folds and lines ran over them. "If you go into the office, on the tippity top shelf in the closet. Push all that junk out of the way, and you'll find a banged up ole box I want you to take care of for me."

"What's in it?" Ailey asked, too curious to wait for Grampa's answer.

"Regrets." Grampa folded his hands together.

"Regrets?" Ailey repeated. "How can a box have regrets?"

Grampa took a deep breath like he wanted to suck in all the air in the room. His grayish brown eyes dimmed. "Years ago, when I was a little older than you, about twelve, I was given a gift." He paused. "But I doubted myself too much to accept it. I was kind of like you. Didn't have the right kind of confidence. Too afraid to really try."

"I'm not afraid—" Ailey started, but the look Grampa gave him said he wasn't fooling anybody. So instead he asked, "What's in the box, Grampa?"

"I'm getting to that." Grampa wasn't a man to be rushed. "You know, over seventy-some-odd years, I've gone in that closet from time to time when everyone is sleeping and opened that box."

"For over seventy years?" Ailey felt his eyes go big.

Grampa nodded and peered at him. "Now remember: What I'm 'bout to tell you stays here. Sammy is the only other person I've ever told."

"Not even Gramma Franny?" Ailey couldn't believe Grampa would've kept anything from her.

"Nope. Not even her. Too embarrassed to let her know I was scared." Then he touched his chest and pressed his fingers against Ailey's. "You and me. Not your momma, your dad, or Jojo. And definitely not King. He ain't never been good at keeping secrets. Though he's a sneaky one, probably already knows."

"I promise." Ailey gave the Cub Scout salute, even though he wasn't a Cub Scout. "I won't tell." And he meant it.

CHAPTER SEVEN

SHOULDA, WOULDA, COULDA

"When I was a little older than you, and my head still wasn't big enough for my ears," Grampa began. "Livin' back in Harlem, I used to eat, sleep, and breathe tap dancing. I didn't do much else. And I was *good* too. But at the time, I didn't think it." Grampa shook his head. "To get change in my pockets and to help out at home, I used to tap at the corner of 125th Street and Eighth Avenue in New York City, steps away from the famous Apollo Theater. You know, where all those great Black entertainers performed. I drew some crowds too, I don't mind telling you. Great day'n the morning, I was *somethin'*. Everybody called me Taps, on account I was always tappin'."

His feet suddenly jumped under the covers as if on a hot stove. He knocked them against the baseboard of the hospital bed.

Ailey stared. Even though Grampa's feet where hidden

54

under the quilt, Ailey knew Grampa was tapping and he never did that when someone could watch. "That doesn't sound like regret."

"Well, it led to it." Grampa became serious then. The sheets went still. "One bright Saturday afternoon I was out there tappin' for the folks strutting by, hoping they'd have the Christian spirit and drop me a penny or two. But, I got more than a penny that day. A crowd formed around me and none other than Mr. Bill Bojangles Robinson himself stepped to the front and started tappin' with little 'ole me. Can you believe it? There he was. The big Broadway and movie star tappin' right there with *me*."

"He was a movie star then?" Ailey stared. He'd seen a few of Bojangles's movies with his mom on TV. She loved ancient films.

"Yep, and one of the greatest tap dancers around. I had practiced all his steps after seeing them during matinees. Just like you do with all those videos and rap stuff you watch." When Grampa looked toward the window again as if he could see his past, his smile fell a little more. "After we finished tappin', a whole bunch of people put a whole heap of money in my hat. And Mr. Robinson gave me his tap shoes."

"He took them off his feet?" Ailey asked.

Grampa laughed. "No, no Jackrabbit. He had them in a satchel and they sure did gleam. When he tapped with me, he was in a pair of real fancy dress shoes though, like he was going to an important affair."

"And he stopped to tap with you?" Ailey said, impressed.

"Yep, he did." Grampa nodded, bringing Ailey back. "And he gave me his very own tap shoes. Said they always brought him luck and were filled with a smidgen of something special."

"Something special like what?"

"No telling, but I got the feeling he was trying to pull my leg and convince me they held some type of magic."

"Really? What kind?"

"Who knows . . . I never saw none of it. Luck neither," Grampa whispered, dismissing the thought. "I told him I couldn't accept them though. Momma Zelda and your great-great Nanna Truth didn't raise me to take no handouts. I always worked for what I got. And I hadn't worked hard enough to have something so valuable."

"But they were from a famous movie star!" Ailey said. "He could've got more."

"Yeah, I know. People said he used to go through more than thirty pairs a year because he did so much practicin' and tappin'. But, still, I hadn't earned them. So, when I kindly refused, you know what he said?"

"No, what?" Ailey leaned in.

"He told me to hold them for a while, and when I was ready, bring them back to him at a theater on West 44th

Street. He wanted me to get up on that stage, put on those shoes, and show him what I had."

"Did you do it, Grampa?" Ailey tugged Grampa's arm. "Did you show him your moves? I know you did."

Grampa's shoulders sagged as he rocked his head. "No, I never got on that stage. When I finally got up the courage, it was too late. Mr. Robinson was gone. The show had been sold to the World's Fair. I took too long. Lost that possibility. And I never got another chance to change my stars."

"Change your stars?" Ailey asked. "How would you have done that?"

"By getting another chance. Changing the outcome. Like *you* can."

"But I can't," Ailey said, tucking his hands in his lap.

"I bet you could if you really wanted." Grampa squeezed Ailey's shoulder. "And if you are fortunate enough to get another chance, you better hold on to it with both hands— strong. And with every bit of heart and grit, you have to seize that possibility."

Ailey sat silent for a while. Then asked, "But how come you waited so long?"

"I was too sure I'd fail," Grampa admitted.

The only light coming into the room was a soft glow of light from the hallway, coming in through the closed blinds in the hospital room door.

"But he told you that you were *good*. You said all those

people on that corner were clapping and putting money in your hat. Why'd you think you couldn't do it?"

"Why do you?" Grampa turned the question back on Ailey.

"That's different," Ailey said. "You were great."

"And you could be too," Grampa said, looking him square in the face.

"Maybe." Ailey, shifted uncomfortably on the quilt. "But Mahalia's better."

"*Pshh.*" Grampa waved his hand in the air as if shooing away dust. "The only difference between you and her is confidence and more practice. Once you have those two things, you're unstoppable."

"But why didn't you have them?" Ailey asked. "Sounds like you practiced *all* the time."

"That's part of my regret," Grampa said. "I didn't believe in myself. I should've gone on that stage and showed all I could do. Your Uncle Sammy never showed no fear in the boxing ring, even with one busted eye. But I never had that same steel. There's no telling what could've happened if I had. Those shoes are a reminder of that failure. And every time I go in that closet and take out my shoe rag and polish 'em, they still shine like the day I got them. But while they shine, if I'm truthful, a little part of me keeps dimming. Those shoes stir up somethin' . . . I'll always wonder—what if?"

"Then why do you keep taking them out?"

"Because I don't want to forget how fear led me instead of courage. Don't get me wrong, there have been so many wonderful things in my life—Franny, rest her beautiful soul, you, Jojo, your mom and dad, but that regret has been pinching on my heart for so long. I can't shake it. I just wish I'd tried. And every time I'm polishing them, I remember that. And that I would never be changing my stars."

"You should've believed you could do it."

"You're right, Jackrabbit, and now I need you to polish them. Not because I want you to carry my regret, but because I don't want you to have your own. This play might seem small now, but giving up on anything you are excited about is big. Too big to ignore." Their eyes met again. "That's why I never want any of you to get too comfortable with that word *never*. I don't want you having regrets like me. It's an awful feeling to know you didn't give the things you love a true try. Promise me you won't give up on anything, especially that play. And promise me you'll keep polishing those shoes."

"But I already told you, I messed up real bad. I fell flat on my face."

"Your face looks alright to me."

"It doesn't matter though," Ailey said. "I can't try out again."

"Who said?" Grampa asked. "Practice real hard and if

there's a way to try again, try. Promise me you will. Don't have regrets like me."

"Okay, Grampa," Ailey promised, wondering why Grampa was making the play a bigger deal than Ailey thought it was. His words worried Ailey a little. Actually, they worried him a lot. Grampa was talking like he was going to die.

"Hey, who dun cut the lights off in here?" The fluorescent lights buzzed as the room was showered in brightness. Ailey had to blink quickly to adjust. Grampa's brother, Uncle Sammy stood in the doorway, a porkpie hat on his head, his left eye patch standing out, begging to tell its story. "Why you all acting like somebody died in here?"

Ailey swallowed and glanced at Grampa. Uncle Sammy stepped into the room, followed by Ailey's parents and Jojo.

"I came here for Jojo's birthday, and here you are laying up in a bed trying to take all the attention. Figures." Uncle Sammy shook his head at his younger brother.

"My party's canceled," Jojo said and slid back onto the bench she'd sat on before.

Mom shot her a look.

"What?" Jojo raised her hands, palms up. "It is, isn't it?"

"Now I told you not to go canceling nothing tomorrow on account of me," Grampa said.

"Okay, Dad. We'll discuss it later, but for now let's figure out what's happening with you."

Grampa turned to Jojo as if Mom hadn't spoken and winked. "Your party's not canceled."

Jojo's smile was huge, and it annoyed Ailey. She didn't even seem worried about Grampa anymore. Then her skinny fingers started hammering against her phone screen and Ailey kept his mouth shut, though he wanted to scream. His head filled with everything Grampa had told him. He had so many more questions, but he couldn't ask them then. He'd promised to keep Grampa's secret. And that was exactly what he planned to do.

CHAPTER EIGHT

DON'T AVOID THE STUMBLE AND THE FALL

Mom rested her cheek against Grampa's shoulder and squeezed her arms around him. "Good night, Daddy. I'll be here first thing in the morning, okay?"

"Don't trouble yourself," he said. "You have a party to get ready for." He glanced at Jojo, winking.

Jojo smiled back.

Mom sighed. "I'll be here in the morning."

"Suit yourself."

Just before Ailey stepped into the hallway, Grampa cleared his throat. "Don't forget," he said, nodding.

Ailey stopped, Jojo bumping against his back. "I won't." Then he couldn't help himself and dashed back into Grampa's arms just as his mom had stood to leave. "I'll take good care of them 'til you get home," he whispered against Grampa chest.

Grampa rubbed his hand high on Ailey's back. "Don't

ever forget. I'm counting on you," is all he said, but those words were almost more than Ailey could bear to hear. They sounded like Grampa wasn't ever coming back home.

☆ ☆ ☆

"Uncle Sammy, you awake?" Ailey rolled on his side, his shoulder sunk deep into the air mattress his mom had blown up at the foot of his bed.

"*Ummmhuh*?" Uncle Sammy breathed.

Ailey could tell he was on his way to sleep or was already there. Earlier, Ailey had lost his courage to ask his great-uncle any questions about Grampa and the tap shoes, but he wasn't sure how many more chances he would have before Uncle Sammy went back home. Ailey rubbed his thumb over the engraving on the back of his Black Panther watch like it was his security blanket. *My superhero. Love, Grampa.* He refastened the watchband around his wrist and pushed the button to illuminate the Black Panther on his wall.

Then in a weak voice he asked, "Were you there when Grampa met Bojangles?"

Ailey wasn't sure his great-uncle had heard him and almost felt relief.

The bed sheets above him rustled, and the light on his nightstand came on. Uncle Sammy peered over the edge of the bed at Ailey.

"How you know about that?"

Ailey shut off his watch. "Grampa told me."

"Did he now . . ." Uncle Sammy squinted his good eye. He didn't wear his eye patch as he slept, so it took almost all of Ailey's willpower not to stare at the watering fogged-over, blind one. "What exactly did he tell you?"

"Everything, I guess." Ailey looked away, not sure if this conversation was betraying Grampa.

"Everything?"

Ailey shrugged. "How come he never tapped again, when Mr. Bojangles wanted him to?"

"He froze," Uncle Sammy said. Wide-awake. Grampa was right, he didn't go around topics. He plowed right through them. *He told straight truth.* "He always froze when it was something important. He'd lose his nerve."

"But he *was* really good, wasn't he?"

"Heck," Uncle Sammy snorted. "He was better than really good. He could've been one of the best."

"You couldn't get him to try?" Ailey propped himself up on his elbow. "He wouldn't listen?"

Uncle Sammy chuckled. "He ain't listened to me since he was ten."

Uncle Sammy squinted at Ailey and raised a finger, poking it at the air like Grampa often did. "Don't be shakin' in your boots. You can be scared, yes, but you still gotta have grit. It's that grit that keeps you going. It won't let nothin' stop you or stand in your way. And he didn't have it. Point is, you can't give up when you get knocked down. You gotta try and stand again."

Ailey couldn't help but feel his great-uncle might be talking about him, too, but he didn't want to think about that.

"But some people just aren't like that though," Uncle Sammy said. They don't keep trying, so they can avoid the fall. But if you don't fall, you might as well not live. I don't know 'bout anybody else, but the greatest feeling is when you get back up off that canvas and win." Uncle Sammy smiled, then it faded. "My li'l brother might've done his fair bit of stumbling, but he *always* avoided the fall. So he never got a chance to win. To see what that other life could've been, one where the thing he loved—tapping—was in it."

Ailey didn't speak, but he thought about Grampa's stars. Uncle Sammy kind of made it seem like Grampa's life wasn't any good with the stars he had. Like he, Mom, Dad, and Jojo weren't part of living. Like the life Grampa had with them wasn't complete. But Ailey knew that wasn't what he meant at all. One of the things Grampa loved was missing. Ailey couldn't imagine what it would be like if he couldn't put words together in his mind to figure things out. Even with his family all around him, he knew a part of him would be lost without his raps.

"So, Grampa misses tapping real bad, huh?"

Uncle Sammy switched off the lamp, and the glow-in-the-dark stickers on the ceiling and walls that mirrored the night sky were the only light in the room.

"I know he does. Like a dried-up pond misses water," Uncle Sammy said, yawning. "If he'd just been willing to stumble and fall . . ."

Ailey couldn't sleep.

A queasiness settled at the bottom of his stomach. It told him he might be worried about the fall, too, but he didn't want to be. He wanted to be brave and try.

He stared up at the glow stickers. Usually he could spend hours searching out the constellations and galaxies he and his dad had spent a long weekend putting up, but that night, Ailey couldn't concentrate. Besides Uncle Sammy snoring louder than a freight train rumbled, Ailey's thoughts bounced from wanting to be the Scarecrow, to wanting to forget it, to wanting to try. But at the center of his thoughts were the tap shoes.

With all the commotion, he hadn't had the opportunity to slip away and see them. But now all was quiet, and he could take a chance.

Slipping out of his sleeping bag, he flopped off the air

mattress as Uncle Sammy's top lip fluttered. Ailey crept to his desk and grabbed his earbuds and iPod Nano, wanting to hear the Crow Anthem one more time. He also pulled on his robe, because the last thing he wanted was to run into Jojo in the hall so she could clown him about his Black Panther union suit with footsies. *She just didn't get how cool the Black Panther was.*

As soon as he opened the door and stepped into the hallway, there she was, headed up the steps, a silk night scarf over her hair. Ailey was just about to duck back in his room when she spotted him.

"What are you doing up?" she asked stepping onto the second-floor landing in her pink plaid pajama pants and a t-shirt she'd made herself that read: *Beauty sleep + me = Fabulous*, with "fabulous" spelled out in pink sparkles. She balanced a plate of Oreos on top of a glass of milk.

"None of your business."

"Well don't even think about going down there and messing up any of my party decorations."

"Nobody's thinking about your stupid decorations." Ailey pushed by her elbow. "I don't want to go to your party anyway. Unlike you, I'm thinking about Grampa!"

He stomped down the stairs hoping she wouldn't say another word.

When he reached the bottom step, he heard the

unmistakable thumping of King's paws on the stairs behind him.

"Oh, come on," he said when King stopped. "You probably already know what's up anyway."

Ailey raced over to the front door, then hesitated, King at his side. He knew it was an absolute no-no to go down to the hardware store without permission, especially at night, *but hadn't Grampa asked him to?*

He slid back the chain and eased open the door. He was down the stairs in less than two seconds, King tramped down behind him.

He was ready to see what regret could look like.

CHAPTER NINE

THE TIPPITY-TOP SHELF

How come rooms always look spookier when you're not really supposed to be in them? Ailey tried to ignore the shadows cast by hanging hammers that loomed large like trolls climbing the wall. The slumbering computer that sounded more like the hiss of a snake than the rattle of an ancient machine. And the gurgling belch of the water cooler . . . Well, Ailey didn't even want to think about that.

But he and King stepped farther inside.

Ailey was on a mission.

He moved closer to the closet. His hand hovered over the knob for a second. Bojangles's shoes were on the other side. The latch clinked and the door scraped the floor as he pushed it open.

Ailey rushed forward and reached wildly for the light cord. With a click, the small space flooded with orangey-yellow light and more shadows. His eyes darted around. The

sounds were fainter now. King stood at the door of the closet.

"Do you know where they are, boy?" Ailey asked him while scanning the shelves.

Stacked boxes of every shape and size towered above him. But on the tippity-top shelf in the corner, two paint cans hunkered down like guards. Ailey knew exactly what sat behind them. He grabbed the stepladder and hesitated.

"Here goes," he said to King over his shoulder.

King howl-whined. Then Ailey started climbing. As he slid the paint cans aside, his nervousness *whooshed* away, replaced by a root beer–rush of excitement.

Exhaling, he pushed the boxes out of the way. An old mustard-colored box with a crumpled corner sat unprotected. A logo on the side read "Matzeliger Shoes. Pampering feet since 1883. New York, New York." King barked, his paws tapping against the concrete floor.

"*Shh*," Ailey warned, pulling the box forward. "You're gonna get us busted."

King groaned.

He yanked off the lid. A ruby-colored velvet bag sat inside. Ailey lifted it out as a disk of shoe polish tumbled onto a cloth at the bottom of the box. Scooping them out, Ailey replaced the lid and shoved the box far into the corner. Then he set the other boxes and guards back in front of it so it was like he was never there.

With the velvet bag tucked in the crook of his arm, he shoved the polish and cloth in his pocket. He hopped off the ladder, turned off the light, and dashed out of the closet. King at his heels. He went to Grampa's workbench where a model of Grampa's dream car, a powder blue '53 Chevy, sat in front of ordered jars and tools. He slid the shoe polish and cloth on the bench remembering how fun it was putting together the model with Grampa. A pinch worried his chest. He wondered if they'd get to make more. He pushed the thought away.

Grampa's secret took its place.

Light from a star-filled night pressed in through the windowpanes. Grampa and Gramma Franny smiled down at Ailey from a framed photograph over the workbench. They hugged under the Lane Family Hardware awning during the grand opening of the store. An orange pickup sat off to the side, since Grampa couldn't afford the Chevy.

Not able to wait a second more, Ailey yanked open the sack.

Inside the folds of velvet, the shoes peeked out at him. His hand trembled as he eased one shoe out and then the other. They gleamed in the starlight flooding the room.

King sat tall in front of him. He sniffed at the shoes.

"Whoa . . . Get back! No slobbering."

Ailey's fingertips tingled as he clutched the plain but

shiny black-brown shoes. He held them out in front of him, turning them this way and that.

"They just look like shoes," he admitted, not sure what he'd expected to find. His eyes ran along the distinct, hair-thin stain that ran down the left tap before he turned them back over. The loosely laced shoes seemed like they were ready to be worn. He couldn't believe Grampa had never tried them. But he wasn't Grampa. Even though his feet would have to grow four times larger to fit them, he dropped them on the floor to give them a try. King gave a low growl and whine, backing up.

"It's okay, boy. I'm not going to mess them up."

King whined again.

As if pulled by magnets, Ailey could have sworn the shoes moved an inch closer to his feet.

"You see that?"

King's head tilted, his panting heavy.

"I know, a person'll believe anything in the dark," Ailey said. "Here goes."

Without another thought, he slipped his feet inside. They felt like any other oversize shoes. It was kind of disappointing. *Shouldn't shoes that held Grampa's greatest regret feel different somehow?*

He wiggled his toes, free inside the leather walls. He tried to lift his foot to tap but nearly toppled over. The shoes were definitely too big. Even when he knotted the laces, their openings were wide. But he didn't take them off. Instead, he started to flow.

Alright, alright, alright,
About to hit the stage like Grampops tonight
But I gotta move slick not to mess up my kicks,
I could tell by the crowd
I'm the one they adore.
And when I leave the stage
They'll be beggin' for more.

"*Ahh*, snap." Ailey rocked his upper body, batting his hand at the air.

He did a little shuffle. Then he flung his arms out, attempting to run in place. If he wasn't careful, he'd send the shoes flying across the floor with one swing of his foot.

The tap shoes almost glowed in the light spilling through the window. With the moon only partially visible, Ailey marveled at the brightness of the stars.

He wiggled his toes in the roomy shoes as he peered outside. The Guiding Star glimmered as if it wanted him to share its spotlight. Then Ailey sucked in a breath. The little star he was sure Grampa called Aida twinkled ten times brighter than the brightest firework. "We don't want

Grampa to have any regrets, do we?" Ailey whispered to Aida, tapping his foot.

"I wish we could help him change his stars." Ailey pretended he could tap like Grampa.

And that's when it happened.

There was a *slurp*.

Then a *sloop* . . .

And a *swish* . . .

Then a *crackle* . . .

The shoe leather hugged his toes and the laces settled into elegant knots.

That didn't just happen. I know that didn't just happen. Ailey stared at his feet, his heart thundering. King scrambled back, barking and growling at the shoes. Not caring who he woke.

Before Ailey could shush him, a tingle flickered up his legs. Twirled about his spine. Spread out to his fingertips.

The walls rippled. The shelves shook. Hammers rattled.

There was a *pop*.

King's bark and the *bzzzz* of a swooping fly got swallowed in sudden silence.

"King . . ."

The shelves, the computer, the workbench, and walls were gone. And so was King. Everything went black, like Ailey had been blindfolded. He tried to shout, but couldn't get the sound out of his throat.

He fell and fell and spun all at once.

There was nothing to see and nothing to hold. His arms and legs kicked and bucked at air.

Then. Pavement.

A shower of sound blasted his ears.

A pinhole of light grew wider and wider. The brightness stung. The blindfold ripped away. Ailey squinted. Standing.

Where am I?

CHAPTER TEN

IS THERE A CIRCUS IN TOWN?

Something was wrong. Terribly wrong.

A crowded street corner came into focus as Ailey whirled around. Sights and sounds pulled his attention: the clopping of horse hooves, the sputter of antique car engines, the constant *weeer* of a fire truck bell. A Black police officer in a long navy blue coat with gold buttons blew on a whistle. His white-gloved hands motioned this way and that as he directed the bustling traffic and a mass of black faces waiting to cross the street. Ailey stood in shock. Rooted to the pavement. Purses and elbows brushed against him on the busy sidewalk.

What was going on? Where was he?

Smoke curled out of what looked like a stove chimney perched on the pavement. The smell of roasted nuts floated to his nose.

"Hot yams, one penny. Get your smokin' hot sweet yams," a man with rolled up sleeves sang.

"A penny?" Ailey said, looking around.

Where in the world was he? And what had happened to King and the hardware store? Panic climbed his chest.

"Whatcha got on there under that fuzzy coat, son? A cat suit?" A man selling five-cent sodas off a cart leaned close to Ailey, moving to touch him.

Ailey jumped back.

"Relax now. I wasn't trying to scare the black off you. I just never seen no threads like that. What you going for?"

Ailey stared, confused.

"Cat got your tongue too?" The man grinned revealing a large gap between his front teeth. "Is it hush-hush?" He leaned close, whispering, eyes darting around.

"Huh?" Ailey had no clue what the man was talking about.

And he was too close. Breathing on Ailey.

"You in a show or somethin'?" The man reached out again.

Ailey jerked back, catching sight of his sleeve.

Then, like a meteor crashing to earth, it hit him. In the middle of a busy street. In what looked like the middle of the day, Ailey stood—for all to see—in his Black Panther PJ's, microfiber robe, and Grampa's tap shoes.

He yanked his robe closed. *Not that it made a difference.*

He had to get out of there.

"You alright there, Slim?"

Slim?

The toothy smile disappeared from the man's face. Ripples curled his forehead. "You look like you need a garbage pail or something. You gonna be sick?"

He fanned Ailey with his newspaper as Ailey took an unsteady step backward.

"No, I'm . . ." Ailey took another step back. His eyes darted around. "I just need to get home."

"And where might that be?" The man continued fanning him.

"Fort Mose Avenue."

"Fort Mose? You sure that's here in Harlem?"

"Harlem?" If Ailey's eyes weren't attached to blood vessels, nerves, and muscles, they would have tumbled out of his head. *Harlem!?!*

"You sure you okay, son? You look like you swallowed a toad."

Before Ailey could reply, his eyes focused on the paper the man had stopped flopping in his face.

Saturday, April 22, 1939.

"1939?" Forgetting his manners, Ailey snatched the paper, shaking it open. "The Wait is Almost Over," the headline read. "Soon the New York World's Fair will open to the world of tomorrow." *What the heck does that mean?* Ailey thought. *The day and month were right, but what had happened to the year?*

"Is this the date?" he asked the soda seller, who now stared at him like he'd escaped the clown routine at the circus.

"This paper. Is. It. Right?" Ailey poked his finger at the ink.

"Son, I don't know how you were raised, but where I come from you don't just go ripping a paper out of a hardworking man's hands."

"I'm sorry, sir," Ailey rushed to say. "But is this date right?" His finger shook over the pitch-black ink of the 1939.

"Yeah, that's right." There was no laughter in the man's voice now. "Why? You got somewhere to be?"

Unable to think, Ailey just stared. The newspaper rustled in his hands. "1939, not 2010?"

How had this happened? And how had he ended up in Harlem?

Tears pushed at his eyes. Panic no longer climbed. It catapulted up his throat. His hands clenched, crumbling the man's newspaper. And his feet itched to run.

Ailey's body was in overload.

"Judging from your brown turning to green, I think you better sit," the man said. His voice softened a bit. "Something tells me you shouldn't be wandering around right now."

"Ailey wanted to object, but he felt his feet and the man's gentle nudges leading him to a stoop next to a barbershop with a red, blue, and white ribboned pole. As it spun, Ailey thought he might lose his tuna sandwich, the hospital's flappy baked chicken, and the Oreos he'd snuck to his room.

"I'm going to get you a nice cold soda off my cart, then maybe I oughta call over a copper or someone to help you on your way." The man stood back looking around.

"Copper!" Ailey's head shot up. He knew that word from old movies. *How in the world would he explain any of this to the police while wearing a Black Panther onesie and a bathrobe?*

And he wasn't going to try.

He had to get out of there.

As if his legs suddenly understood something his head still worked out, he hurdled himself off the stoop and ran, nearly knocking people over as he went.

"Hey!" the soda seller called after him, but Ailey blocked him out.

He had to find a way home.

CHAPTER ELEVEN

NOT IN UPPER DARBY ANYMORE

Ailey's gaze whizzed one way, then the other.

A woman selling scarves, handkerchiefs, and ties out of a suitcase followed him with her eyes. He quickened his steps and rushed past a man in a white cap and bowtie pouring red syrup on a snow cone. "1-2-4-5¢" was painted on the side of his cart. Another man leaned against a storefront window that read "Leon's Thriftway." Chewing a toothpick, his eyes tracked Ailey, suspicious. Ailey felt like everyone stared.

He couldn't get off those streets fast enough.

At the next block, he slowed, not sure where to turn. Two women sat behind a long table piled high with clothes. Over their heads, a wooden cross was nailed above a sign hanging from an open window. *Good Hope Mission Previously Loved Clothing Sale* was painted in blue block letters.

Stacks of neatly folded pants, shirts, socks, and hats filled the table. A row of polished, but well worn–down shoes lined up straight. A pair of tan tweed pants lounged over the edge of the table, a rock holding them in place.

One of the women trapped Ailey with her stare. A funny grin pulled at her lips, a mash-up of a smile and a grimace.

"Don't be shy, child, we don't bite." Her eyes roamed up the length of Ailey's body—taking in his robe and the dye-printed boots on his pajama legs. "And by the looks of things," she continued. "You might be in need of what we have. Seems you done come outside in your union suit. And the good Lord done seen fit to turn you our way." Laughter sprinkled her words as the other woman rocked her head from side to side—lips pursed. "You might want to come grab some clothes, or carry your hind parts back home and start your day all over."

Go back home . . . Ailey wished it could be that easy.

Bashful, he inched closer to the table, thinking about the vinyl imprint of the muscular chest design on his pajamas now hidden under his robe. A shirt might be needed.

"Those there are forty cents, cost you seventy-nine at Sears. You got any money?"

Ailey knew the answer, but he shoved his hands in his pocket anyway. *Just like he thought . . . not a coin or dollar.* Then his fingertips brushed against the corner of a folded piece of paper. He pulled it out. The Scarecrow's monologue. He shoved it back in his robe pocket and knocked against his iPod and earbuds. He didn't dare pull those out. He couldn't even begin to explain them.

"I guess that answers that." The woman said looking over the tops of her glasses when his hands left his pockets empty. "But being the good Christians that we are, I will heed Proverbs 21:13 and will not close my ears to the cry of those in need, and child, you are definitely in need."

"Really?" Ailey sighed.

"You probably oughta grab yourself a pair of knickers or pants too. Can't have you running 'round in just a shirt and your peculiar union suit." She leaned forward. Her glasses perched at the end of her nose as she examined his microfiber bathrobe. "Something tells me this isn't a coat." She shook her head. A *tsk* left her lips. "Lawd, children today."

"I think this stuff might be too big." Ailey held the clothes she gave him up against his body.

"Sorry, suga, but I think everything else in the children's pile might be too tight. And you don't want buttons poppin' so you wind up back in your union suit."

In a snug cubby space under the stoop, he took off his robe, put on the shirt, buttoning it quickly. When he started wrestling a pants leg over a shoe, he stiffened. He stared at the cloth twisted around the snitched-up laces. Bojangles's shoes, snug on his feet.

"Oh my goodness . . ."

They really are magic.

"Child, you alright in there?"

"Yes." He tugged the pants on, almost splitting them in the process. He rushed out of the cubby shoving everything else in the pockets of his new, slightly oversize pants. The earbuds flopped against his leg as he tried to cram them deeper in his pocket.

"Thank you again for all of this." Ailey nodded toward his new outfit. "It was very kind of you. Will you take this as a trade?" He held out his robe. "My mom says don't just take without giving in return."

"Oh . . . well she's a wise woman, but I'm not exactly sure what we can do with this." As she held it up, Ailey hustled away.

"Thank you!"

Not feeling as much like a circus clown as he did before, Ailey thought about what Grampa had said about Bojangles's shoes. "There wasn't nothin' special nor lucky in 'em for me."

But he was wrong.

Suddenly, Ailey got one of his ideas.

He stopped at the edge of the sidewalk, clicked his heels together three times, and whispered. "There's no place like home. There's no place like home."

But nothing happened. Not even a sparkle or a shimmer. It wasn't like in the book.

"Whatcha doing over there, son?" said an old man leaning out a second-floor window.

Ailey almost jumped out of his clothes. "Nothing . . ."

He dashed farther down the street. He tried to remember everything Grampa had told him about the shoes.

"Bojangles had said they held a smidgen of something special."

They might not have shown it to Grampa, but they had sure showed something. And Ailey wished they'd do it again.

"I use to tap on the corner of 125th and Eighth Avenue." Grampa's voice splashed through Ailey's mind, clear as spring water. Up the block, he spotted the street signs. Eighth Avenue. *Could that be it? Was Grampa out here somewhere?* Excitement bubbled in Ailey's chest. *Which way was 125th Street?*

He barely noticed the man selling roasted peanuts, or the flock of boys perched on a nearby stoop. He hustled down the street, his head up, searching out the street signs. When he saw the number 125 staring back at him on a street pole, he nearly tripped over a kid sitting on a dining room chair shining shoes in the middle of the sidewalk.

Once Ailey reached the corner, his head whipped from side to side. People moved all around him. Smoke whirled in the air. Old-fashioned cars rattled down the street. So much to see, but no sign of Grampa.

Ailey's excitement slipped. *That would've been too easy.*

CHAPTER TWELVE

SWEAT 'ROUND YOUR COLLAR

"**H**ey, you!" a boy yelled.

Ailey turned just as the caller hopped down from a nearby stoop. Three boys—his shadow.

"Why you passin' so much time on my corner?"

Ailey checked over his shoulder. He was sure the kid wearing a black derby hat tilted deep, hiding his right eye in shadow, slick-like, wasn't speaking to him. Everything about the boy said he was used to being the center of attention. From the medals dangling on his coat pocket to the funny pieces of cloth he wore over his shoes that Ailey had seen in old pictures where men wore fancy clothes.

"What you looking around for?" the boy asked. When Ailey glanced around again, the boy nodded, "Yeah, I sure is talking to you."

"I wasn't—" Ailey lifted his palms.

"You *was*," said the boy. "I'm King and this here's my

throne." He gestured around him, striding over to Ailey with a deep limp to his stride like a wounded animal. Then Ailey realized it wasn't a limp at all, but some strange strut that included a hop, a little skip, and a glide, as if he were on a dance floor. One of his hands rested in his pocket while the other swung free to the bounce of his shuffle. Ailey might have laughed if he hadn't been so nervous.

They kept coming closer.

Ailey's feet squirmed in Bojangles's shoes. They didn't look like they wanted to offer Ailey directions.

"Please take me out of here," he begged the shoes. He craned his neck up to the sky, then down at his feet again, not sure which way to beg. "I promise I won't unscrew the bathroom faucets and fill them with Kool-Aid powder, or accidentally leave my remote control tarantula on Jojo's pillow, or freeze cereal and milk and leave it out for Dad. And I absolutely promise not to stick another one of my helium birthday balloons in the toilet and close the lid, especially when Grampa needs to pee. Now, please, please, please: There's no place like home!" He brought his heels together again wishing like Dorothy.

"What you mumblin'?" King asked as he neared Ailey.

Before Ailey could respond, he heard clapping and cheering. Then silence. Then the distinct sound of someone tapping.

He spun around and there, across the busy street, as the crowd parted a sliver, the back of a young tapper came into view. His arms swung fast, and his legs stomped even faster.

Ailey took a step closer to the curb.

"Hey," called King. "Don't walk away when I'm talkin'."

Ailey heard King, but he was too busy trying to see the boy across the street.

"Don't pay him no mind." King's voice was as gravelly as sandpaper. "He ain't got skills like me."

Then, unexpectedly, Ailey heard clopping behind him. He didn't want to turn away from the boy, but he did.

The kid who called himself King was tapping.

Ailey had never seen anyone move his feet so quick. King's neck was stiff, as if attached to a pole like the Scarecrow. But as his feet slapped against the pavement, like a ruler against a board—*thwack, thwack, thwack*—his body teetered as if off balance. Ailey thought King might topple over any second. He couldn't understand how King's body could be so rigid while his feet pounded out a thunderstorm. King's lips smacked against each other like he kept the beat of a song in his head. His feet were a blur of brown leather.

When his taps competed with even louder applause from across the street, Ailey turned back, wanting the crowd to break apart once more enough to glimpse the tapping boy again.

"Hey." The thunderclaps behind Ailey had stopped.

"What's the matter with you?" A strong hand yanked Ailey back. "You got a problem with my tapping?"

The group of boys closed in tighter. A boy in an aviator cap with swinging earflaps and an old camera dangling on a strap around his neck snapped an image. "Yeah, don't *igg* my man," the boy said. "You don't like his taps?" His voice was high like a whistle. Ailey gulped down a nervous chuckle. King narrowed the space between them, his friends not far behind. Even though they were on a wide-open street, Ailey felt smashed against a wall.

"No, it's . . ." Ailey pedaled back, feeling someone's foot underneath his heel a second before he crunched down. "I mean, yes . . . no. Sorry. I mean I liked it," he added, a nanosecond before he got shoved off one of the boy's toes.

King loomed over Ailey like a mighty wave about to crash. "Well which is it, Slim?" King flicked Ailey's collar as Ailey steadied himself.

Why did people keep calling him, Slim? Ailey wanted to back away and run, but he remembered how Grampa always said, *Look even the meanest devil in the eye. Don't show no fear, no matter how much you want to skedaddle. Don't let 'em see that sweat 'round your collar.*

"My name's not Slim." Ailey drew to his full height, which hardly reached their elbow. His eyes focused on King. "It's Ailey. And I *do* like your tapping."

"Yeah, you right. Your name's not Slim." King's chin

jutted out as he scanned the length of Ailey's body. "How's the view from down there, Ducky?"

Ailey raised a little higher on his toes. He tilted his chin up, inches away from the older boy's chest. "It could be better."

There was a hushed silence, then an eruption of laughter.

"You're all right. You know that, Ducky?" King held his hand up for a high-five. Ailey reluctantly hit it. "Even though you look like you ran out the house tryin' to play mister with your pop's threads, you a'right." The boys around Ailey chuckled and snorted as King nodded toward Ailey's too big, secondhand clothes. Ailey couldn't imagine what they would've thought of him in his bathrobe and union suit.

For the first time, Ailey realized *everyone* was dressed for church. No one wore sneakers or jeans or t-shirts, just slacks, ties, suspenders, button-down shirts, and sweater vests. Some of the boys even had on *suits*! The girls wore dresses and white ankle socks with their hair in plaits and pigtails, looking like Jojo ready for Sunday school. The outfits were nothing like the sweatpants and shorts he was used to seeing on Saturday mornings back in Upper Darby.

"You tap?" King pointed down at the tap shoes on Ailey's feet. "Um . . ." Ailey covered one foot with the other, not sure what to say. Then loud applause sprang through the sky like firecrackers. Everyone looked, including Ailey.

"There he goes again, trying to show off." King sucked air through his teeth, waving his hand as if it could erase all the clapping. "He ain't got nothing on me. You dig?" He knocked Ailey's shoulder just as the crowd parted enough for Ailey to see the face of the tapper who had turned toward the street.

Ailey nearly stepped off the curb into the busy roadway. King snatched him back. "Whoa, Ducky, ain't you got no sense in your head? You want that copper over there callin' a meat wagon when you go splat under some bucket's wheel?"

Not really hearing or understanding anything King had to say, Ailey tittered, trying to right himself as he pointed across the street.

"That's Grampa."

CHAPTER THIRTEEN

THE ONE THEY CALL TAPS

"Come again? What you mean that's your gramps?" King and his friends followed the direction of Ailey's finger. "Who you pointing at?"

"Ah, oh, nobody," Ailey said, dropping his hand. "I thought I saw my grampa. But it wasn't him. Nope." Ailey shot them a sideways glance, then turned back to the boy on the opposite corner. "I gotta go. My . . . um, my dad needs my help. Yeah, um, my help." Before the lie was fully formed, or anyone could stop him, Ailey rushed into the street with the tangle of pedestrians directed by the policeman's whistle.

For a second, he forgot all about the tap shoes and getting back home.

He just wanted to see Grampa.

When he got to the other sidewalk, he slowed. People knocked against him and others brushed by, trying to avoid a collision in the chaotic stream of walkers. Ailey stared at the boy. His head tilted down, sweat beaded at his temples. People clapped the boy on his back, then drifted in different directions. Ailey ducked under someone's arm and squeezed past an elbow for a better look. The boy looked about Ailey's age, with brown skin the same tone as Ailey's. His ears curled, poking out as if they belonged on a bigger head. It had to be him. *Who else would it be? This was his corner.*

Ailey pushed through the crowd impatiently. And before his sense caught up with his mouth, he shouted. "Grampa, it's me, Ailey."

The boy gave him the same look the guy with the soda cart did. The woman at the used clothes table did. And the boys across the street did. But Ailey didn't stop.

"I can't believe I'm meeting you," he said, words tumbling from his mouth. "I mean *young you* because I already know *old you*. But you don't like me calling you old. You like *wise*. But anyway, when I landed here, or fell here, or whatever, I was freaking out, I mean really freaking out. Then I realized the shoes brought me here. They're really magic, Grampa." Ailey kept rambling despite the looks he was getting—from everyone. "When I got here I had no clue where I was, or why. But now I know. It was to find you."

"Find *me*?"

"Yeah," Ailey went on, moving even closer, ignoring everyone passing around them and the boy's puzzled expression. He was sure once Grampa heard his story, all would be fine.

"That was righteous, kid. Gimme some skin." A man in a three-piece suit knocked the boy's shoulder, extending his hand. "You got moves, kid. Real moves."

Ailey dipped under the man's arm. "I can't believe it's you."

"I think you got the wrong one, Slim." The boy stared at Ailey like he was that escapee from the circus again.

"It's not Slim, it's Ailey, remember? Why does everyone keep calling me Slim?" Ailey reached for the boy's sleeve. "You named me. But I guess that doesn't happen for a while."

"Yeah, okay," the boy said, pulling away. He grabbed his hat, coins jingling. "Whatever you say, Slim." He moved past Ailey.

"No, wait! Where are you going? I came here for you. I think to help you. That was my wish, Grampa . . . I guess it was a wish." Ailey rushed forward, almost on the boy's heels.

"Grampa?" The boy leaned back. "Why you keep callin' me that? You fall off a turnip truck or something? I'm not your Grampa. Heck, I ain't nobody's Gramps. Maybe you ought to get along." The boy shoved his change into his pants pockets and turned his back on Ailey, striding away.

Ailey watched, stunned, as the boy got folded into the crowd. Ailey wanted to push through and run after him, but he knew he was already one step away from scaring him off for good. The longer he stared, the more uncertain of

everything he became. Then, he realized he'd forgotten the most important thing—to ask his name.

Ailey couldn't believe he'd been that close and had just let him go. But what was he supposed to do? No one was going to believe him.

He wasn't sure how long he sat on the step near where the boy tapped. His hands on his chin, staring straight ahead. But he didn't know what else to do or where else to go. Luckily, King and his friends had wandered back to their stoop, a girl on King's arm, forgetting all about Ailey. Trying to find calm, Ailey soon found himself nodding to an imagined beat.

> *What am I doin' in this time, in this place*
> *I don't feel welcome and I don't feel safe*
> *Lookin' for Grampa, tryin' to change his fate*
> *Hoping I'm on time and not too late.*
> *Like Dorothy from Kansas, I'm just simply lost.*
> *Harlem movin' so fast I just wish it would pause*
> *Truth be told, I just wanna go home*
> *In a city full of people, but I feel so alone.*

Ailey felt hopeless. He knew he couldn't go around telling people he was from the future—not even Grampa.

And he definitely couldn't mention "borrowed" tap shoes and a "smidgen" of magic.

Stay calm, he breathed.

Discouraged, he closed his eyes and kept rapping. His left leg bouncing.

> *Like Grampa I now understand regret*
> *Stuck in this time just tryin' to get back.*
> *I was tryin' on the shoes 'cause I thought they were cool*
> *Dancin' and rappin', just caught in the mood*
> *Truth be told, they really looked sweet*
> *But now I wish they would've never ever, ever touched my feet.*

As minutes stretched into an hour, he tried not to let his panic build anymore. He twisted the end of his watchband. Then flicked the watch face. The hands of the Black Panther had stopped moving, as if future time had stopped.

He wracked his brain for all the movies and books he'd read and seen about time travel. A mental checklist formed of everything he should or shouldn't do.

> *   *Don't start with "I'm from the future."*
>
> *   *Don't panic when you panic*
>
> *   *Find the right clothes . . .*

But his mind drew a blank when it came to how people got home.

Focus, he shouted in his head, *focus*.

It was still early; however, soon it would get dark. And besides the time he'd fallen asleep on his roof, which really didn't count, he'd never been away from home late at night before, alone.

Think, Ailey, think.

His left leg bounced again. The tap shoe clinking. He pressed his elbow hard into his knee to stop it. Then a little farther down the street someone called out, "Eh, Taps, man, you 'bout to lay it out again?"

Ailey locked onto one single word—Taps.

Wasn't that what everyone called Grampa?

Ailey looked around wildly.

Striding down the street, close to the stoop where Ailey sat, was the same boy in his odd knee-length dress pants and maroon argyle socks. Suspenders peeked from underneath his light gray suit jacket. A bow tie and a burlap sack strapped to his back completed his outfit.

Ailey could do nothing but stare. It *was* Grampa. *There couldn't be that many twelve-year-old boys called Taps in Harlem.*

CHAPTER FOURTEEN

A DEAL IS A DEAL IS A DEAL

"Yeah, I'm gonna do my best." The boy they called Taps responded to the person who'd shouted out to him.

"Alright, Jack. Get to it." The older boy waved over his head and continued down the street, bopping to a beat no one else seemed to hear.

"Oh," Taps said as he turned, nearing the stoop. At first, he looked at Ailey like he was that escapee from the circus again, then he looked at his feet. "You again? You got this corner now?"

Ailey kept staring. He saw Taps's lips moving, but he didn't really hear the words.

"'Cuse me." Taps stepped closer—cautious—like Ailey might be contagious. "You tappin' here?" This time he pointed toward Ailey's feet.

Ailey followed the direction of his finger.

"*Ahh*, no. Just sitting." He wished he could hide the shoes.

"You mind?"

It took Ailey a second to understand what Taps was asking.

There was so much Ailey wanted to say. He didn't want to make another mistake though. So, he simply shook his head.

"Cool." Taps sat down on the steps next to him and pulled off his burlap sack. He took out a pair of tap shoes that had seen better days. It looked like another pair bulged in the bag, but Ailey couldn't be sure.

Can we both have a pair of Bojangles's magic taps? Ailey glanced again at the bag sitting on the stoop between them.

"Okay then," Taps said. "I'll leave you to your thoughts. Looks like something's stirrin' inside you." He swung the straps of his burlap sack over his shoulders and headed toward the corner.

"Huh? What?" Ailey rushed to say, realizing Taps was leaving again. Ailey hopped up. "I'm sorry for before. I didn't mean to freak you out. I haven't fallen off of a truck."

"It's cool, man. Long as you don't start talking it again. Deal?" Taps was already shuffling his feet and swinging his arms capturing a beat. The sack leapt up and down as he tapped.

Ailey breathed out, relieved. Now he just needed to find another way to convince Taps that he was Grampa.

☆ ☆ ☆

Ailey couldn't take his eyes off Taps as he danced. And as he moved in closer, other people crowded Taps, too, like they knew they'd get a show. Young and old, blacks and a few whites huddled around him. Then Ailey spied King and his friends still across the street, on their stoop, staring his way. Ailey pushed deeper into the growing crowd.

The tempo of Taps's *rap-a-tap-tap* pulled everyone in and didn't let go. Just as the crowd was lost in Taps, Taps was lost in a world of his own. Just him, his rhythm, and the pavement. No people. No cars. No sounds other than those of his own tapping.

Ailey couldn't believe how easy he made his *pa-tap-tap-tap* look. While King's feet had slammed against the sidewalk, Taps's glided over it. The sound was rhythmic. Like the beats Ailey heard when he rhymed. They bumped against his chest like a set of drums.

He didn't know a whole lot about tapping, but he recognized skills.

Ailey stood a little taller. A little prouder. *That was Grampa.*

The rhythm of the taps slowed to the beat of a single drum. Taps's face held no expression, only focus. He ran in place, his arms at his sides. *Pa-tap-tap-tap.* His legs swung out and in, doing jumping jacks. *Swish-swish, swish-swish.* He stepped forward, then stepped back. *Click-clack, click-clack.* The patter of his simple movements was louder than even King's thunderstorm. People threw coins in a hat that rested on the sidewalk, and one woman wrapped in a fur shawl dropped in a dollar bill. Ailey smiled. *Taps could buy twenty sodas with that.*

As Taps clacked out his final *clickitty-clack-clack-clack,* an explosion of cheers and applause zipped through the crowd. Everyone pressed in on Ailey, reaching for his grandfather, wanting to wish him well, just like before.

This time Ailey didn't push in or crowd him. But when the last onlooker left, Ailey lingered.

Don't mess this up. Don't mess this up. Please don't mess this up, he warned himself. *You made a deal.*

Taps grabbed up his hat and went back to the stoop. He poured the money onto a handkerchief and tied it in a tight knot. Dusting off his hat, he paused, staring at Ailey's shoes again.

Ailey tucked one behind the other, unable to hide them.

"Nice taps," Taps said. "Not many wear wood anymore. Where'd you get 'em?"

Ailey glanced at the lump in the burlap sack strapped to Taps's back. "Um . . . around." He tried to sound as casual as possible, but heard his own voice shake. "You were awesome," he added. "I've never seen anyone with moves like yours."

Taps shrugged. "There are a lot better."

"I don't believe it," Ailey said. "I haven't seen 'em."

Taps swung his floppy newsboy cap in the direction of Ailey's shoes before he slapped it on his head, adjusting it until it sat perfect. Not too low and not too high. His ears poked out under the brim. Ailey smiled. "So," Taps said still breathing a little heavy. "Why don't you take a turn?"

Ailey felt his face go hot and his smile dropped. "I don't really tap."

"Then why you wearing tap shoes?"

Ailey glanced away. "It's a long story."

"I got time."

Ailey hesitated then looked at Taps. "I made a deal, remember?"

Taps stared back, studying Ailey. "In that case . . . what kind of dancing you do? I know you dance. So, can you tell me that?"

Ailey exhaled, his cheeks lifting. "I like hip-hop."

"What *hop*?" Taps asked. "Is it somethin' like the Lindy-Hop?"

"The who?" Ailey said before he could catch himself. "Maybe."

Taps plunked down on the steps and took off his shoe. He wiggled his toes out in front of him. A neat maroon stitch crisscrossed over the big toe of his sock. A familiar pattern that closed holes in Ailey's socks too.

"You should try tappin'. It might suit you. Besides, you already got the shoes," Taps said. "It's all about practice."

"Grampa—I mean someone I know always says that."

The corner of Taps's mouth turned up. "He's a smart man. Listen to him. Practice."

Ailey squirmed a little at these words. Then without really knowing why, he blurted out, "Yeah, practice probably would've helped with this play I tried out for at school. I crashed and burned. Bad."

"That's even more of a reason to practice now."

"It's already over. Besides, it's not really about tap. I mean, it's not really about dancing at all, but I wanted it to be."

"Doesn't mean practicing now would be a waste. Practice is never wasted. So here you go. Your stage is right here." Taps spread open his palm. "I'll even leave if you want some space.

"No. You don't have to do that." Ailey rushed to say.

"Then just try," Taps encouraged. "You might be great."

Just like you. Ailey bit back the words he wanted to say.

Taps took off his other shoe, then looked back up. "I'm Benji by the way." He raised his chin. "Named after Benjamin Banneker. The famous astronomer."

Ailey grinned. "My middle name's Benjamin."

"Really? My Nanna Truth thought it'd be clever to name

me after a man who always stayed among the stars." Benji shook his head. "But most people 'round here just call me Taps." He offered Ailey his hand.

Grampa, I knew it was you, Ailey thought but said, "I'm Ailey." His heart pounding.

"Interestin' name, Ailey." Taps's hand continued to hover.

Ailey hesitated, but didn't shake the long, slender fingers that were the same chestnut brown as his own. He knew it was ridiculous, but he was afraid that if they touched, something strange might happen like one of them might ignite or maybe disappear. He didn't know why he thought it, but he wasn't ready to leave this moment just yet. "I was named after a famous dancer."

"We both got big shoes to fill." Taps glanced down at his outstretched hand, then back at Ailey.

You got that right.

Slowly, Ailey slid his hand forward and held his breath. He closed his eyes tight when he felt Taps's warm calloused palm. Their hands moved together, then Taps relaxed his grip. Ailey took a moment before he opened his eyes, letting go.

Nothing had happened.

No sparks flew, no clouds parted, and no heavens rumbled.

Ailey was still there, and glad to be.

CHAPTER FIFTEEN

CHICKEN'S NOT MY NAME

"**Y**ou wanna share some of my sandwich?" Taps asked Ailey as he pulled off his sack. "I think it's leftover pork chop. You haven't had pork chops 'til you've had my gram's."

He's talking about great-great Nanna Truth, Ailey thought, marveling at the fact.

"She makes the best butter pound cake too. Even drizzles it with sugar icing—*mm-mmm*." Taps pulled out his lunch, neatly wrapped in wax paper, and placed it on the step between them.

"You sure?" Ailey asked. "I mean you don't even know me. And I was saying a lot of strange—"

Taps held up his hand. "I was taught not to eat in front of someone if I wasn't offering them none. And I don't know 'bout you, but I'm starving. And I wasn't telling you to get off the stoop when you got here first. Though I haven't seen you 'round here before."

"I'm new," Ailey said.

"Thought so. I know most everybody that comes around," Taps said. "You mind grabbing something from the soda man over there?" He pointed toward the man and bicycle cart at the curb. "Here." Taps dug in his pocket and flicked a coin through the air. "You pick the flavor."

Ailey stared at the nickel, wishing he'd had a couple coins in his own pocket. Grampa always said repay kindness with kindness however you can. Then the image of saying goodbye to Grampa in that hospital bed crashed into his mind.

"Ailey?"

"Huh?" Ailey blinked, realizing he hadn't moved.

Over at the cart, glass bottles filled with orange, red, purple, and other colored liquids fenced a slab of ice. Ailey picked his favorite: root beer.

When he got back to the stoop, Taps had spread out the bandana and divided the sandwich in half. He'd even split the cake in two and gave Ailey an equal piece of his banana.

"Dig in," Taps said, before taking a huge bite of his half of the sandwich.

The bread pressed like a sponge in Ailey's hands, clinging to the pork chop that rested between the slices. His first bite was heaven, as was the second, and by the fifth, it was gone. Ailey nudged the stuck bread off the roof of his mouth with his tongue and licked his fingertips.

"Told you, ain't nobody alive make a pork chop sandwich

like my Nanna Truth," Taps boasted. "Try that cake. Bet you never had nothin' like that either."

Ailey bit into the spongy-sweetness and instantly thought of home and his mom's kitchen. His mom's pound cake was the best, but this was better than the best. He could eat this cake every day for a year and still want more.

"I wasn't lyin', was I?" Taps asked eyeing him. "Ain't nothin' like it."

Ailey licked his lips, finishing the last piece when King and his friend with the aviator cap and camera strutted up 125th Street toward them. They barely waited for the men in front of them to pass before they cut over to Ailey and Taps.

"Thought you had to get on home?" King interrogated Ailey.

"I, um . . . did. I do." Ailey licked his finger. "But I was already too late to help. So, what's the point in getting in trouble now, when I can hold off and get in the same trouble later?" He was surprised how easily the excuse rolled off his sugarcoated tongue.

"I hear that, Ducky." King nodded. "No point in spoiling a perfectly good Saturday morn with a butt whoopin', right Zee?" He nudged his friend.

Zee chuckled. "Yeah, you ain't lyin'."

"What you up to, Benji?" asked King.

"Nothing much."

"You oughta add some of my tricks to your show." King

shuffled his feet, throwing his arms out to the sides like he was drowning in water. *Pwish-wish-sish.*

It actually looked kind of cool.

"I don't have a show," Taps said, holding the last of his banana close to his mouth. "Besides, I think I'll leave all the fancy tricks to you, I'm still learnin'."

"Get outta here, Slim. You always actin' like you too good for these slick moves." King went back to spinning his arms and hopped over one leg with the other. *Cli-pac, cli-pac, cli-pac-pac-pac.*

Even though King's moves were pretty good and daring, they didn't have the smoothness of Taps's. King was a little rough, or as Grampa always said, *he needed a li'l' spit and polish to make him shine.*

"I'm not too good for anything," Taps corrected. "I'm just tryin'."

"Whatever, Jack." King sucked his teeth.

"You do more than try," Ailey added, sick of King's bragging. "A whole lot of people put a whole lot of money in your hat because they thought you were great."

"So, you made decent bacon?" King looked down the block.

"I did all right," Taps said. A glob of banana pushed out his cheek as he chewed.

"Back a few days ago, a fella put a Lincoln in my can."

King swept his finger around the brim of his hat and puffed up his chest.

"You lyin'. Ain't nobody ever give you no nickel note," Zee chirped. But he snapped his beak shut when King sent him a look that could cut through lead. Even Ailey pinched his lips together tighter, and he hadn't been the one talking.

King lifted his shoulders and turned back to Ailey and Taps. "Well, he *almost* did . . ."

As King bragged, Taps reached down and laced up his shoes.

"So, you gonna join me now? Show me how you *think* it's done?" King dared. *Clickitty-clac, clickitty-clac, clickitty-clack-clack-clack.*

"Nobody can show you nothin'." Taps got up and jingled his leg as crumbs fell.

"Well, let's see what you workin' with."

"I already told you. I'm just tryin' to tap."

"Well, then tap." *Clickitty-clac, clickitty-clac, clickitty-clack-clack-clack.*

Taps lingered on the step. "Ain't you got somewhere to be?"

"*Naw.*" King touched his chest. "I'm free as a bird. Gots all day."

Taps sat back down fumbling with his laces. "I'll wait a bit. The corner's all yours."

"Oh, you're giving me permission now? Thank you, kind sir!" There was a bite of heat behind King's words. "Didn't know you owned this corner. But I wasn't askin' permission anyway. Besides, it sounds to me like you chicken."

"Ha-ha." Zee shook his head. "*Bwok-bwok-bwok*."

A plate of worms slithered in the pit of Ailey's stomach. *Was this what "shaking in your boots" looked like? Was Uncle Sammy right, did he really have trouble tapping when people watched?*

The first time Taps tapped, no one had been paying attention at the beginning, but now eyes locked on him from the start, and he knew it.

Is that why he'd flopped?

Ailey wondered if he was even more like Grampa than he'd thought.

"Whatcha scared for?" King chuckled.

"Yeah," Zee mocked. "*Bwok-bwok-bwok*."

"Clap your trap," Taps warned. "I ain't no chicken. I'm just waitin' 'til my food settles."

"Don't blow your wig, man." King waved him off with a snicker. "You don't have anything I want to see anyway. I got all the moves I need." King leaned forward, his right leg tapping out. *Plackitty-plac-plac. Plackitty-plac-plac.*

"Come on Zee, let's blow. Leave these strange birds on the stoop. They ain't up to nothing."

"Yeah, they ain't up to nothin'," Zee added, snapping a photo of Ailey and Taps.

Ailey watched as they got lost in the crowd. Every part of him wanted to defend Taps. Let the world know he was great. But Ailey realized the believing had to start with Benji.

CHAPTER SIXTEEN

ONE CLICKITTY-CLACK AT A TIME

"How come you didn't show 'em?" Ailey asked a minute later. "He was trying to say you aren't as good. You're better than him."

"Don't pay him no mind. He's harmless." Taps batted his hand at the air. "Like Nanna Truth says about people like him, don't give their showboatin' your time. They strut around like peacocks, flashing their feathers because no one looks otherwise."

"But people are looking your way. Because you're good. More than good," Ailey said.

Taps got up. "Says who?"

"I do," Ailey said. *And Bojangles.*

At first, Taps didn't say anything, like he hadn't heard Ailey. He just stared off as cars rumbled and horse-carts clopped past. Then he said, "You wanna join me? Learn some taps?"

"Sure." Ailey bolted off the stoop, wanting as much time with Grampa as he could get. "If I'd known some of your moves, they would've been begging me to play the Scarecrow." Ailey spun around.

"Is this *Scarecrow* a tapper too?"

"*Naw*, but he's really cool. The coolest part in the play if you ask me."

"What happened?" Taps asked. "How come you think you messed it all up?"

"When I needed to, I couldn't remember a single line. That's why."

"You practice?" Taps asked, his feet lazily tapping.

Ailey didn't need to respond. From the look in Taps's eyes, he already knew the answer.

Ailey pulled out the sheets shoved in his pocket. "These are some of the Scarecrow's lines."

Taps focused, scanning the page.

"I couldn't remember any of them when I needed to." Ailey sulked.

"*Awww*, you can get this, no sweat," Taps said, rubbing his hands together.

"It's too late now," Ailey said.

"It's never too late. Stand next to me and watch." He tapped out the first words of the scene. "Psst! Psst! Psst! Hey little girl! Hey! Hey!" *Du-du-du, da-ta-ta-da, da-da* went his feet. Then he continued, adding the next lines.

"Hey," Ailey said, following along on the paper. "That's pretty cool."

"It's just finding the beat of the words."

"Oh, I get it, kind of like when I put rap lyrics to a beat in my mind."

"Rap?" Taps eyebrows pulled together.

"Yeah, rap." Ailey smirked. This, he could talk about. "It's like poetry set to music."

"So, it's singing?"

"No . . . it's more like talking. But you have to have some rhythm behind it. You can't be stale and whack. No one wants a stiff rhyme. Like if I started *flowin' on this street*." He jiggled his hand back and forth like he rolled dice in his open palm. "*Tryin' to catch some beats.*"

> *Rappin' is about rhymes, fast or slow*
> *In any direction it's all in the flow*
> *See you gotta have swag,*
> *And you gotta have style*
> *To spit your truth nice and loud*

"Hey, that sounds real neat. You just make it up right here and now?"

"Yeah." Ailey turned a little shy.

Badap-dap-dap. Taps caught Ailey's rhythm. Then he

motioned for Ailey to tap it out too. "Think of your hands and feet connected by a puppet string," Taps said. "You're already playing out the beat when you shake your hands or when you rap. Now add your feet."

"I don't know," Ailey said. "That's where things get kind of complicated. I can't remember the lines I need to know. And then my toes don't wanna speak."

"Look." Taps pointed at Ailey's feet. "Don't think. Just let it happen."

He did exactly what Taps showed him—again, and again, and again. "Check that out," he said, a couple minutes later. His foot tapping along.

"Faster," Taps encouraged when Ailey had gotten the basic step. "And keep saying the lines out loud." He padded out a simple *rap-a-tap-tap*, then changed it to *pa-tap*, *pa-tap*, *pa-tap*, like he jumped rope when he recited the next line.

"No way." Ailey backed up, shaking his head. "I could never do that like that."

"Don't ever say 'never'." Taps looked at him, a stern expression crossed his face. It was an expression Ailey was all too familiar with at home. "Nanna Truth says that's a sure-fire way to close off your possibilities."

"My grampa says the same thing," Ailey added, thinking about their earlier conversation, then realizing their deal. "My bad . . ."

"No worries." Taps brushed it off.

"Wise man knowing the same wisdom as my gram."

Ailey's lips turned up.

"No slackin'. Get back to it."

Ailey didn't grumble. He just tried.

Tap my feet
And find the beat.
My boy Taps
is here to teach.

☆ ☆ ☆

Taps didn't groan when Ailey messed up, and he didn't laugh when he stumbled. He simply changed the way he showed him a step until Ailey got it right, just like Grampa would.

"I'm useless at this," Ailey said a while later when he kept tripping up on the same step and line from the Crow's Anthem. "I don't think this whole tapping-and-learning-lines thing is for me . . .

How can I tap my feet to the sound of a beat?
And not spit my rhymes at the same time.
My head gets clogged and my feet turn cold
And that's when disaster starts to unfold . . .

Maybe I should forget the tapping and just dance."

"Nothing wrong with that. But it sounds like you need

the lines too. Just stop thinking so hard and let your feet take you where you need to go."

Tic-a-tac-tac, tic-a-tac-tac, tic-tic-tac-tac, boom, boom. Taps's feet padded against the pavement. His head slightly bent and his arms hung loosely at his sides, like he strolled in place. His expression glazed over. No longer focused on Ailey.

Ailey stepped back watching him, amazed by all the sounds coming from such little movement. Soon other elbows pressed in, as they had before. Another crowd marveling at Taps.

His *bip-bo-bip* had everyone smiling, swinging their heads, and clapping. In no time, people stared, two rings deep, then three. Taps's *clickitty-clop* had people stomping to his beat.

Then there was a faint *clic-clac, clic-clac, clic-clac* in the distance that wasn't coming from Taps's feet. People toward the back of the growing crowd rumbled and whispered. Their grins nearly split their face in two. Then the crowd parted.

A man with a bright white smile, big, round eyes, and cheeks that sat like balls in his cocoa-brown skin stood and gazed at Taps, who was lost to everything around him. The man placed a bag on the ground at the rim of the crowd. Then for a moment, folded his arms, nodding along. No one said a word as Taps moved, unaware of anything or anyone but his taps.

Stepping in front of him, the man became Taps's mirror.

Rapitty-tap, rappitty-tap-tap clicked Taps. *Rapitty-tap, rappitty-tap-tap* echoed the stranger. Some people chuckled, while others seemed to hold their breath as the stranger followed Taps's lead.

Pa-tac, Pa-tac, Pa-tac-tac rang out, as if coming through a loudspeaker. Becoming even louder with two sets of feet.

"Alright now, son," the man said, giving Taps back the stage. His head bobbed in time.

Taps was still lost. *Buduk-buduk-buduk-duk.*

Everyone applauded and whistled as his arms whirled. Whipping to a frenzied beat. Building momentum.

Click-itty, click-itty, click-itty-clac, Clac-clac hammered Taps's feet as he coaxed out the last notes. The sound echoed, imitating the speed of a woodpecker. Only then did he raise his head. Sweat clung to his skin. His feet stopped, midair. The man with the bright white smile lifted his hat toward him. Taps's lips parted as if he wanted to speak, but nothing came out as his feet landed softly against pavement. The man tipped his hat. Taps stared. His manners automatic. He gave a slight bow. The crowd leaned in as one.

Ailey stiffened.

It all started here. The moment Ailey had wished to help change. The moment Grampa met Bill "Bojangles" Robinson—the star.

The moment that started his lifelong regret.

CHAPTER SEVENTEEN

THE MEETING OF GREAT FEET

Taps and everyone else were glued to the man standing in the middle of the circle—not troubled by all the gawking. Ailey would have melted with so many eyes on him. After all, he almost had at auditions. But he knew this was different. Bigger. It was about Grampa.

The sounds of the city seemed to quiet, as if waiting along with everyone else to see what the man would do. A hush swept through the crowd.

Anticipation.

Excitement.

Eagerness.

All bounced through the air. And Taps stood at the center of it all with his idol, the man Ailey was sure was the King of Taps.

Pit-pat, pit-pat went the man's left foot, tracking Taps with his eyes. An easy smile curved his lips. *Clic-clac, clic-clac* went his right. He nodded for Taps to follow. A strange look

119

took over Taps's face. Like he wanted that same black hole that Ailey's memory had fallen into to come get him. He glanced around, not settling his gaze.

His body rigid and still.

Clic-clac, clic-clac, clic-clac, the man's feet said again, not troubled by Taps's lack of response.

"Come on," shouted someone. "The Mayor's waitin'."

"Yeah, get to it," another called.

The man they called the Mayor put his finger to his lips, still smiling. The crowd quieted down. But Taps didn't move.

"What's goin' on here?" came a voice bursting through everyone else's. Ailey recognized it at once. King broke through the crowd across from Ailey, Zee at his side.

"Oh, snap," he said. "Mister Robinson."

"Yep." Zee raised his camera. *Click.* "That sure is Mr. Bojangles."

"*Shh,*" a woman with a peach shawl hissed.

King's lip curled, then he looked where everyone else's attention was—on Taps.

"You got it, son," Mr. Bojangles encouraged. "Go for it."
Pli-tac, pli-tac.

But Taps did nothing. Ailey knew exactly how it felt to have all those eyes on him. He wanted to rush in and help, but didn't know how. This was why he was here, and he didn't have any idea what to do.

Then King pushed forward. "That fool always chokes when people watchin'. Let me show y'all how it's done. Mr. Bojangles, sir, you aren't likely to forget me." *Clappitty-clappitty-du-dunt.* King shuffled his feet, slapping the sidewalk.

"That's it," a voice yelled as he picked up speed. A couple people applauded. But even more had to move out of King's way as he moved around the crowd, elbows out.

Mr. Bojangles quieted him with a shake of his head. "It's his moment, son," he said. He never took his eyes off Taps, but it was clear he was speaking to King.

King stopped, looking like someone snatched his new bike right out of his hands.

Unfortunately, none of this knocked Taps into action.

"Put some heat under your feet, Jack. We ain't got all day," someone complained.

"Take your time, son," Bojangles said. He casually clicked against the cement. Heel to toe. Heel to toe. "Close your eyes and feel that beat. Get rid of the noise. Turn off the radio."

At first, Taps just stared ahead, blinking. No other part of him moved.

"Go on, close 'em." Bojangles urged. "Nice and tight."

When he finally did, Bojangles tapped. *Clop-itty-clop-clop. Clop-itty-clop-clop.*

When a few people started to forget themselves again and cheer, Bojangles pressed his hands down as if pushing down the noise. Sputtering cars seemed to silence as Ailey closed his eyes for a split second, hoping. After a while, Taps's thumb brushed against his thigh keeping to the rhythm. "That's it," Mr. Robinson mouthed.

You got this, Grampa.

Then Taps's knees bent a little and slowly he shuffled his feet, keeping them close to the ground. When he raised them a bit higher, the taps came a bit faster. And a little louder. *Bibitty-bop-bop. Bibitty-bop-bop.*

"Alright. You got it now." Bojangles nodded his head, joining in. He cupped his hands behind his back and did a sort of skip-step around Taps, as if taking a stroll. *Clipitty-clop, clipitty-clop, clipitty-clipitty-clic-clic-clop.* His smile brightened his eyes. And he whistled. Taps didn't seem to notice. He'd found his world again. Lost to his taps, his eyes opened, but they locked onto something beyond the crowd.

Bojangles mirrored Taps's movements again.

When Taps went *Ka-tap-tap-tap.*

Bojangles went *Ka-tap-tap-tap.*

When Taps slapped out *Rap-itty-tap, rapitty-tap-tap-tap.*

Bojangles slapped out the same.

The crowd kept growing. Soon all Ailey could see around him were rows and rows of smiling brown faces spilling into the street.

After a while, Mr. Robinson hunched over playfully, holding his back as if it ached, as old men often do. But he kept right on tapping and the crowd erupted in claps, hoots, and hollers. Taps didn't seem to care. But Ailey noticed the same couldn't be said for King. Scowling eyes pelted fireballs at Taps.

Taps kept dancing.

By the end, he and Bojangles banged out a blustering tap that sounded like it could shake any building.

Ailey's ears rang from the taps, claps, and roars of the crowd.

When Taps and Bojangles's feet settled, their chests still leapt up and down.

"You sure laid iron, Jack," someone hollered.

"You did indeed," Bojangles agreed, pushing his hat back on his head, dabbing his forehead with a handkerchief he'd pulled from his pocket. "You're more than all right, son. You got a name?"

Since Taps's mouth was slow to form words, Ailey blurted, "Benji, sir. His name is Benjamin. But he's known as Taps."

"Taps, huh?" Bojangles looked up as if considering the name.

"Yes, sir. Mister Bojangles, sir," Taps finally said.

"I can see why." Bojangles nodded toward Taps's feet as he strolled close to the crowd opposite from Ailey. "Well, there's something I'd like to give you." He bent down and reached into his bag.

Ailey gasped.

This was it!

Everyone followed Bojangles's every move, including Taps.

"These have always held a smidgen of magic for me. Maybe they will for you too." He pulled the shoes out to *oohhs* and *aahhs.*

Taps blinked, his hands at his sides. Bojangles held out gleaming but scuffed shoes. Identical to the ones on Ailey's feet.

"Thank you, sir," Taps squeaked out. "But I can't." A ripple of confusion traveled around the crowd. Taps ignored it. "My gramma told me I shouldn't take anything I didn't earn."

"Boy, you better not be a fool. *That's* what she'd tell you now," advised a thin man pointing a toothpick at Taps.

Bojangles chuckled. "Well, in my book you earned 'em. Would you agree folks?"

Mm-hmmm.

Taps's lip curved at one corner. "I really do appreciate the gift, Mr. Bojangles, sir. But really, I wouldn't feel right."

"Oh, come now, Jack," a man in a dark suit warned. "You can't be turnin' down the Mayor."

Ailey couldn't understand why everyone kept calling people "Slim" and "Jack" and why they kept saying Bojangles was the Mayor. He didn't think major cities had Black mayors yet in the 1930s.

"I'll take 'em if he won't." Someone laughed.

"Tell you what," Bojangles said, ignoring everyone except Taps. "You hold on to 'em for a bit, treat 'em real good. "And when you're ready to get up on my stage, I'll take 'em back. Deal?"

"Your stage?" Taps asked, unsure.

"Of course," Bojangles said. "Come on over and show me what you got."

"I wouldn't turn down the invitation," a woman in a green dress teased.

Laughter rang out again.

"Alright, alright." Bojangles placed the well-worn black-brown shoes in Taps's hands. Scuffed and shiny, just like Ailey's. "You come see me now."

Taps nodded, bowing his head slightly. "Yes, sir. Thank you, sir."

Tipping his hat to the crowd, and then to Taps, Bojangles grabbed up his bag and, just like that, divided the sea of people. Ailey could only see the top of his hat as people swarmed him as he headed away.

Taps was a statue, peering down at the shoes in his hands.

King grumbled off to the side. "I could've done better."

And Ailey just stared, trying to make sense of it all. He knew the shoes brought him to that exact moment for a reason. A reason he now understood. Grampa had to get on that stage. But a worry ball rolled around his stomach, getting larger as each second ticked by. He knew the shoes had brought him to Harlem, but what would happen if he couldn't fulfill what he was sent to do? *Would they still take him back home?*

CHAPTER EIGHTEEN

ABSOLUTELY NO STATIC CLING

Taps hadn't said a thing since Mr. Bojangles had left. He'd simply wandered over to the steps cradling the tap shoes. Ailey thought he might be in shock, and couldn't blame him. He had tapped with the best.

"You were great," Ailey said, stepping closer to him. "I mean, can you believe it? Mr. Bojangles was just right here. Tapping with you." Even though Ailey didn't know much about Mr. Robinson, he could tell by the size of the crowd, King's expression, and Taps's bewilderment that he was a very big deal.

Taps kept shaking his head, looking down at the gift resting in his lap. The toes of the scuffed shoes turned up slightly as if staring at Taps too.

"What are you going to do with them?" Ailey asked.

"He's gonna bring 'em back tomorrow. That's what he's gonna do," King interrupted, hovering near the stoop.

"Heck, if it was me, I'd bring 'em back right now. But he ain't as smart as me."

"Nope. He ain't," Zee added.

Taps raised his head, as if just realizing King and Zee were still there and that Ailey had placed his hat bulging with money next to him.

"Well?" King asked. "Whatcha gonna do? 'Cause if you're too scared, I'll go see the Mayor. I got an open invitation to the Broadhurst anytime I want." He reached for the tap shoes, but Taps swung his knees so they were out of reach.

"Stop callin' me scared," Taps demanded. He nestled the shoes deeper in his lap. "I'm not scared."

"Sure did seem it over there." King nodded to where Taps and Bojangles had danced.

"*Bwok-bwok-bwok*." Zee flapped his arms.

"Leave him alone," Ailey said, stepping between King and Taps. "You're just mad Bojangles wanted to dance with him, not you."

"If the Mayor had seen me tap, he would've been tappin' with me." King puffed out his chest.

"He did see you," Ailey said.

"Yeah," Zee chimed in. "He did see you. And didn't pay you no mind."

Before Zee could shut his own mouth. King swatted the

camera around his neck, sending it flying toward Zee's chin.

"Watch it," King warned, then turned back to Taps. "You gonna mess it up anyway. You're no better than a block of ice when people are hawkin'." He froze, stuck in a pose, and then huffed, pushing past Ailey. He did that *hop-skip-limp strut* again.

Zee scurried behind, rubbing his chin.

"Ignore them," Ailey said. "They're just jealous. You won't be shaking in your boots if you go to see the Mayor, will you?"

Taps's eyes narrowed and his face had gone tight. "Who said anything about shaking in my boots?"

Ailey swallowed hard. He couldn't mess this up. So, unlike Uncle Sammy, he didn't plow straight ahead. Instead, he asked, "Why do they call him the Mayor? Was he elected?"

Taps shook his head. "You don't know much, do you?" His expression relaxed a bit though. "Not on paper. He did have a badge and a special pistol from the police, but really it's because people love him, so we *made* him *our* mayor—the Mayor of Harlem. We didn't need no vote."

"Wow," Ailey said grinning. "You tapped with a movie star and a mayor in one day. That's pretty cool."

Taps finally let a smile creep across his face.

"So, what are you going to do with the shoes?" Ailey didn't plow, but he tried to tiptoe straight ahead.

"I'm gonna bring 'em back, that's what."

"Now?" Ailey offered, fingers crossed behind his back.

Taps scowled. "No. He's probably not even there now."

Ailey hesitated. "You're probably right. But soon though, right?" His voice was more desperate than he wanted it to sound. But if he couldn't get him to the Mayor, Taps wouldn't be the only one with regrets.

Taps moved off the step, settling his cap. "I think I'll trilly," he said instead of answering Ailey's question.

Ailey had no clue what he meant, but when Taps gathered up all his stuff and stood like he was leaving, Ailey understood loud and clear. He *was* leaving.

But he couldn't. Not yet.

Ailey had a wish to help fulfill.

"Can I come?" he asked before he could stop himself. "I mean, you want company walking some of the way? Not sure I'm ready to go home just yet." *Or even know how to get there.*

"Your old man really gonna lay into you, huh?" Taps asked. "Well, come on then." He started down the street, not needing an answer. Ailey ran to catch up.

"So, what's your old man like anyway?" Taps asked once Ailey reached him.

"He's pretty cool. He owns a hardware store with my—"

"He got a roarin' temper or somethin'? Or does he just get mean when he's on that hooch?"

"Hooch?"

"Yeah, hooch." Taps tipped his head back, cupping his hand, and pretended to drink.

Part of Ailey wanted to say, *no way, not my dad*, but another part of him knew Taps would start wondering why he wouldn't just go home.

Home. With all the excitement of the last few hours, Ailey hadn't thought much more about it. But now, as he noticed the sun setting and streetlights and storefront signs flashing on, he started to worry again. About Grampa, his health, and how frightened everyone probably was since he'd disappeared in the middle of the night. There was no way to tell how long he'd been gone, but he knew his mom had probably awakened every neighbor, called SWAT, the Air Force, National Guard, FBI, Marines, and even animal control by now.

Looking down at the shoes, he wondered if he'd ever see any of them again.

"You alright, man?" Taps asked, slowing. "You look like you swallowed a spoonful of cod liver oil or somethin'. And that's nothing nice."

Ailey snapped out of it when Taps touched his sleeve. Still no sparks, and no static cling.

"I'm sorry, what?"

"You know, cod liver oil." Taps stuck out his tongue and gagged. "Tastes worse than tar."

"Never had it."

"You lucky," Taps went on. "The stuff's awful. My gram is convinced it's the cure for anything from stomachaches to warts. But between you and me," he leaned close, his sack knocking against Ailey's shoulder, "Anything that cures warts, I'm not all too sure I want to swallow. You dig?"

Ailey was trying to concentrate on what Taps was saying, but couldn't. His mind whirled and a quiet panic took over again. He couldn't leave Taps until he got on that stage. *But how was he going to get him there? He couldn't follow him all night. And he had no clue how the shoes worked. Would they keep him there for hours or days, or forever? He just didn't know.*

Wanting to stay with Taps or figure out a way back home was like deciding whether he liked stargazing with Grampa or Dungeon Avengers more, you just couldn't compare the two—pears and grapes. Apples and oranges.

"What's up, man? You sure is lookin' funny." Taps's smile faded.

"No." Ailey met his eyes and forced a smile. "I'm good."

"It won't be that awful, will it?" Taps asked. "I mean you really think he's gonna lay into you bad?"

Ailey scrunched his brow like he had a bad headache. "Who? What . . . oh," Ailey said. "No, that'll be okay. I got other stuff on my mind."

"For me, a day of tappin' and a night of skygazin' washes all my heavy thoughts away." Taps tilted his head back.

Ailey nodded. "Skygazing always does make us feel better."

"Who's *us*?" Taps asked. "Thought I was the only one who called it that."

Ailey glanced up at the sky, then back down at the shoes. "Nope. Me and my . . . friend do too."

"I sit on the fire escape, staring out at the night, searching," Taps said, his neck craned back so he could study the sky. "It's clear out there: not a lot of lights. Street lamps around me always seem to be out." He chuckled. "Everybody always asks what I'm searching for, and I tell 'em: stars." As he spoke, his head remained back. "And you know what they ask next?" Taps turned to Ailey. Ailey didn't answer even though he knew. "They ask how come I call it skygazin' if I'm looking for stars? And you know what I tell 'em?" A wide smile broke out across his face. "I tell 'em—"

"The sky is home to all those stars." The words were out of Ailey's mouth without thinking. He'd said them so many times himself whenever anyone asked about his skygazing with Grampa.

"So, you *do* know?" Taps chortled. "I *knew* there was somethin' 'bout you I liked. From the start, I knew you and me was like-minded. Cut from the same cloth."

Ailey grinned in agreement. Now he just needed to figure out what might get Taps to shake off his fears and try.

133

CHAPTER NINETEEN

TWINKLE, TWINKLE LITTLE STAR

"So, you like acting and being on stage?" Taps asked Ailey as they headed up 125th Street.

Ailey shrugged. "Never actually done it before. But anyone who saw me bomb at tryouts would probably tell you I should give it up right now."

"I doubt that," Taps said. "Sounds to me like you just need a little more practice and some attitude, like: *I can do this.*"

"Grit, huh?" Ailey wanted to find that attitude and grit for both of them. "If I knew what you know, there'd be no stopping me."

Taps brushed away the compliment. "We all got stuff we know and stuff we don't. That's why it's good talkin' to new folks. Find out about people and things you didn't know. Like rap. I wish I could do that rap thing you do," Taps admitted. "Seems like you need to be full of confidence and attitude for that."

"I never really thought of it like that," Ailey said. "I don't know . . . it just flows off my mind. You know, kinda like the beat flows outta your feet."

Taps smiled with his whole face.

They walked along in silence for a while and passed a poster offering fried chicken and waffles for seventy-five cents. Ailey's stomach groaned.

"Well." Taps stopped suddenly. "Here's where I say goodnight." He peered through a store's front window. "I wanna get something nice for my family with some of the unexpected change I got."

Ailey read the words painted on the glass: *Black Swan Records*. He knew his dad would love that place, but he couldn't think about that now. The night couldn't end so fast. *But what was he supposed to do? Follow him inside?*

"You're an interesting one, Ailey." Taps held out his hand again.

Think! Ailey shouted to himself. *Think!* But he couldn't.

Reluctantly, he reached out and shook Taps's offered hand, not sure what else to do. And again, no sparks, no thunderclaps, and no rumbles. When Taps tried to let go, Ailey held on a few seconds too long. And as Taps twisted his fingers free, Ailey jumped forward and hugged him. He knew it probably seemed strange, but he couldn't stop himself. A second later, coming to his senses, he dropped his arms. Not looking at Taps he said, "It was real nice to meet you and watch you tap. You're amazing! Everyone should get to see what you can do."

At first Taps just stared. Then he said, "Nice to meet you too, little man. Don't forget to keep practicing. You're a natural. Got it in your blood, like me."

Ailey gave a half smile. "But I kept tripping up."

"That's nothing a little practice can't fix. You should see me when I'm tryin' somethin' new—awful."

Ailey found that hard to believe. The grampa he knew was good at everything. He studied Taps, not sure he'd ever see him after this.

"Come back by the corner again sometime, okay? I'm always around," Taps offered, as if reading Ailey's thoughts. "I wanna hear heaps more about that hip-hop and rap." And try to *learn how to flow*." His neck swerved like Ailey's when he started thinking about a new rhythm.

Taps chuckled. Then his smile fell. "Hope things don't get too bad at home tonight."

"Oh . . . yeah, I'll be okay. But thanks." It took all of Ailey's willpower not to follow Taps into the store. "See you," he said after Taps was already gone.

"Now what?" Ailey sighed searching the street.

After a few seconds hovering around the doorway like an abandoned puppy, he tried to make his way back to the corner he'd started on that morning. If he could find it. He pushed back his sleeve, his watch coming into view.

The hands on the Black Panther still didn't move.

He pressed the button that controlled the growl. A low grumble roared from his wrist. *At least something still worked,* he thought, pressing another button to awaken the familiar hologram across the sidewalk. But he quickly clicked it off and dropped his sleeve, realizing that it wasn't one of his best ideas. A busy street in 1939. *How would he explain that?*

The farther Ailey roamed away from Taps, the more he felt alone. And the more worried he was about not being able to do what he thought the shoes had brought him there to do—help get Taps on the stage.

Streets were filling with couples in fancy suits and dresses. Upbeat tunes bounced about through open doors and windows. Lights got brighter as the sky grew darker. And Ailey was no closer to helping Grampa.

The panic that taunted him earlier no longer just teased. It nearly suffocated him. Everything around him seemed strange, loud, bright, and unfamiliar. His panic rose. Musical notes on the outside of a club blinked as he spun around, frantic, almost knocking a couple off the sidewalk. Bojangles's shoes pinched his feet, and since they weren't helping get him any closer to changing Taps's stars, all he wanted was to kick them off.

"You okay, little man?" A couple stopped in front of him. They reminded Ailey of his parents decked out on date night. "You lost?"

He didn't respond.

"Where you trying to get?"

Ailey shook his head and wandered away, knowing they couldn't help him. He felt them watching him, but he didn't turn back. Instead, he kept on, tilting his head up. All he saw was a haze of light, almost as if it were daylight. Then he stood as still as stone. *Where were all the stars?*

He concentrated hard. Maybe there was another way home. Maybe the only way out wasn't just getting Taps up on the stage. Although he really wanted to help Grampa, he also didn't want to be left on the streets of Harlem— alone. He wanted to be tough, but he wasn't. He wanted to go home. *Maybe there's some way to change things from the present.* But he knew that was even more unlikely than a hotel giving a room to a kid alone with no money. It looked like there was no way to avoid spending the night in the cold under an empty sky.

Wait! Maybe that was it, he thought, his gaze rocketing up again. *Hadn't he been looking at the stars when everything went haywire? Hadn't he made his wish while staring at Aida's twinkling light? Maybe it wasn't just clicking his heels; maybe he needed the help of the stars.*

Something Grampa always told him flew into his mind. *The beauty of stars is that the same ones we see over Upper Darby, I saw as a boy in Harlem.*

Could it be that simple? Ailey wondered, hopeful. *Did he just need to wish on the right star?*

CHAPTER TWENTY

SHADOWS AREN'T THE ONLY PLACES MONSTERS HIDE

Simple, it was not. Nothing about finding Aida's Star, the star Ailey had wished on, the little one near Venus that might make everything right, was simple to find, especially in all this city light.

He knew his stars, planets, constellations, supernovas, nebulae, and galaxies. But there weren't enough patches of dark for his eyes to adjust. Aida's Star was nowhere to be seen.

He wandered, his head cocked back, hoping for a break from the lights. The hands of his Black Panther watch still didn't budge. He wondered what time it was at home and what everyone was doing. He was sure his mom was up, and that there'd be no peace in the neighborhood until he was home.

As much as he didn't want to be the bull's-eye for his mom's worry, he also didn't want to be away from Grampa for even one second more. With the way he'd been talking in the hospital, Ailey didn't know how much more time they'd have together.

Then, he remembered the look on Grampa's face when he talked about the shoes. *No, he had to find a way to help him erase his regret.*

"Eh!" Ailey jumped as a hand gripped his shoulder, interrupting his thoughts. "Hey, hey, whatcha got goin' on there, Slim?"

Ailey jerked his head back. A man with glassy hazel eyes stared down at him. His smile almost swallowed his face. Or what Ailey could see of it. His hat dipped low over his eyes. He wore the most peculiar looking off-white suit. It seemed like football pads sat underneath its shoulders.

"Where you headed, Slim?" the man asked. A long feather in the side of his wide-brimmed hat caught the breeze as he leaned close.

In his pointed-toe shoes, the same off-white as his tapered pants, the man looked straight out of an old gangster movie. His suit coat swept past his knees, and a long, double-strand gold chain attached to his belt loop dangled down to his leg. The other end getting lost in his pocket.

Ailey leaned away, but the stranger's fingers dug into his shoulder.

"You a boy of few words. I like that." The man sucked in air like he was slurping through a straw.

Nails bit into the fabric of Ailey's shirt.

"You got a name?"

Ailey didn't answer. This man gave him the creeps. Ailey rotated his shoulder, hoping to shrug free, but the man just tightened his grip. "You're hurting me. Let go," Ailey complained, squirming.

The man stepped closer. His hold still firm.

"No bother," he said, as if Ailey hadn't spoken. "Names aren't all that important anyway. But you can call me Bumpy. Everybody does."

If Ailey had thought about laughing at a name like Bumpy, he quickly thought better of it when the stranger shoved a loose fist inches away from his face. A gold ring with a large square diamond sat on his finger. "I need you to run something down there for me. A ruff in it for ya." Bumpy pulled out a quarter and nodded behind him toward a side street.

"Let go of me," Ailey pleaded. He twisted around, hoping someone would see or hear him, but Bumpy pushed him into the mouth of the dark alley. A black cave surrounded by a sea of light. He hovered over Ailey, blocking his view of the people and their view of him. Ailey tried to scream, only to have his shouts muffled by buttons and a chest that smelled of eye-tearing cologne, B.O., and cigar smoke.

"You drive a hard bargain, kid." Bumpy held Ailey at

arm's length and bent forward. His suit jacket nearly grazed the ground. "I'll give ya seventy-five cents. How's that sound? Ya want tuh make some easy bread?"

"I don't want your money." Ailey shouted, free of Bumpy's smoky jacket.

"*Awh*, don't do me like that." Bumpy's smile didn't quite reach his eyes. "It'll be real quick. I just need ya tuh—"

But before he could finish his sentence or reach in his pocket, Ailey swooped his body down and then back up again. He kicked out as hard and as fast as he could. The toe of Bojangles's nice, hard shoe made contact with bone. Bumpy hopped back, grabbing for his shin.

"You little weasel," he shouted, his voice strained.

As Ailey stumbled backward, Bumpy's arms tore through the air, reaching for his sleeve, trying to snatch him. But Ailey was too quick. Or so he thought. As he took off running, his arm got tugged back. He thought Bumpy had gotten hold of him again. But in all his squirming, Ailey's arm had gotten hooked between the double strands of the gold watch chain. As Bumpy lunged for him, Ailey yanked his arm forward. The chain snapped free. A pocket watch sailed through the air, swinging on the chain as Ailey ran. It bounced off his thigh and crashed to the ground.

Ailey's heart pounded faster than his feet hitting the pavement. He dashed across the sidewalk, not looking back.

He tore off down the street and nearly got clotheslined by a couple holding hands.

"Hey, slow down, son. Where's the fire?"

The couple lifted their arms just as Ailey crouched underneath them.

He kept running. His heart slammed against his chest, and his feet carried him faster than they ever had before.

"Hey, stop that rascal!" Bumpy shouted scooping up the pocket watch as he ran. "He tried to steal my gold watch!"

Ailey begged his legs to move faster as Bojangles's taps smacked the ground. He had no idea where to go.

"Wait 'til I get my hands on you," Bumpy spat.

If Ailey's foot hadn't smashed into Bumpy's shin, Ailey was certain he would have been ground turkey already.

"Leave me alone," Ailey screamed. "I don't want your watch."

When he dared to glance back, he saw Bumpy get knocked sideways by a tide of laughing couples leaving a restaurant. His hand swung over his head. "Someone stop that kid!" His off-white suit coat flapped at his sides like a cape.

CRASH!

Ailey smacked right into three young women, arms locked, strolling around the corner. The women yelped as they tumbled down. Ailey scrambled over their skirts.

"Sorry," he breathed, catching sight of Bumpy gaining ground.

Ailey took off again, leaving them on the sidewalk in a heap.

Bumpy was still coming.

"Ailey, is that you?" a voice called from near a storefront.

Ailey looked around to see Taps standing off to the side, a brown paper bag in his hand.

"Help," Ailey screeched. "Please." He glanced back but dared not slow down as Bumpy flew past one of the young women who had made it off the ground, knocking her down again. His sharp-toed shoe landed in her hat.

"That's right," Bumpy shouted, "Hold him."

Catching up to Ailey, Taps gripped Ailey's arm. "What did you do?"

Ailey could hardly get the words out between breaths. "He wouldn't let go. I kicked him."

"He's madder than a hatter 'cause you kicked him?" Taps asked tucking the paper bag under his arm, running too.

"No," Ailey breathed. "It was an accident. His watch came off. He wouldn't let go. It smashed to the ground. It wasn't my fault."

"It don't seem like he agrees." Taps glanced back. Then he yanked Ailey's arm, pulling him down one side street and then another.

"I got you now," Bumpy said, suddenly behind them, barreling down an alleyway.

Ailey panicked and ripped away from Taps.

"What are you doing?" Taps yelled, but it was too late. Ailey was already headed into the street.

"Stay away from me." Tears streamed down Ailey's face as Bumpy pushed past Taps.

"Watch out," Taps screamed as Ailey turned, just in time to see bright white lights hunkering down on him.

Then he felt strong arms yank him back.

As if in slow motion, Ailey's head tilted back, and he finally saw the night stars he'd been searching for. Screeching tires, burning rubber, and smoke twisted in the air around him. The truck skidded to a stop.

"I got you now," Bumpy said. Ailey kicked wildly.

The driver's door of the truck swung open. "Have you lost your ever-loving mind, running in the street like that?"

"Hey, what's happening here?" A tall police officer stepped up on the curb just as the burly truck driver reached Ailey and Bumpy.

Bumpy instantly let go of Ailey, raising his hands. He backed away quicker than Ailey could blink.

"Nothin', officer," he said. "We all good here."

"What's your name, son?" the cop asked Ailey, keeping a watchful eye on Bumpy.

Ailey couldn't find his voice.

"His name's Ailey, sir" Taps said for him, pushing forward as people slowed to see what was going on. "That man was chasin' him. Tryin' to hurt him."

"I was doin' no such thing, officer. The kid don't have his facts straight. We just playin', right, Jack?" He nodded toward Ailey, but Ailey still didn't speak. "Things just got a bit outta hand, but it's all good now. Everybody's okay. You don't have to trouble yourself none."

Ailey wanted to scream *Liar!* But he could hardly catch his breath.

"Why don't you two go on home? Watch out for him," the officer ordered, as Taps led Ailey away. "He's had quite a scare. Now for you," the officer said to Bumpy, his voice like steel.

☆ ☆ ☆

"Why'd you do that?" Taps asked Ailey when they'd gotten a block away. "You almost scared my naps straight." Taps smoothed his hand over the hair peeking from under his cap.

Ailey still couldn't find his voice, but he wasn't sure what to say even if he could.

"I think you better come on home with me for a bit. Settle your nerves, 'cause you're white as a sheet, and even though I don't know 'em, I bet your mom and dad—black like me."

Even with all that had just happened, for the first time in hours Ailey felt some of his panic fall away. He wasn't going home, but he was going to family.

CHAPTER TWENTY-ONE

IT WASN'T A MIRAGE, IT WAS FAMILY

"**N**ow what you say your name is again, suga?" Taps's gramma asked when she stepped through the kitchen doorway into the foyer. Two thick gray braids wound around her head and settled in a tight bun at the back of her neck.

Grease popped on the stove behind her. The spices on the frying fish brought a song out of Ailey's belly. He hovered by the front door, in the dim light off the entryway.

"Ailey," he squeaked, sweat moistening his collar.

"Speak up, child. I can't rightly hear you with all the singing happenin' on that stove."

"Ailey, ma'am," he said a little stronger, though he felt as if his throat were closing.

"No *ma'ams* here. Call me Nanna Truth, like everybody else. I'm Benjamin's gramma." She took four purposeful strides across the dining room, around an oval table covered with a lace cloth. A vase of yellow daisies sat in the middle.

She paused to center the vase, even though it already looked pretty centered. "Well come on in. We won't bite." She beckoned Ailey forward. "Unless you're a chicken thigh, then I can't help you 'cause I'm partial to those myself."

Skin creased at the corner of her eyes when she smiled. A wide gap showed between her front teeth. *She's my great-great gramma.* She cupped Ailey under her arm and patted his sleeve. Her body felt snug as a fuzzy robe. She pulled him deeper into the warmth of the room, where there was more light.

"I'll be," she said after a moment. "If you ain't the spittin' image of a young Sammy. Come on out here, Zelda, and look at this."

A sewing machine stopped humming in the distance. A pretty woman with a curled bang, as if a roller still sat in it, stepped out of a room down the hall. Black bat-winged framed glasses dangled on a chain around her neck. "What is it, Momma? I'm almost finished Madame Walker's dress. And I still haven't pinned for Mr. Cuffe's suit."

"That'll hold. Come on here now."

Ailey would have known Grampa's mom anywhere. Grampa had tons of pictures of her. One sat in a frame by Gramma Franny's, back at home. Ailey stared at it every time he went into Grampa's room.

"Ain't he Sammy's twin?" Nanna Truth said. "Lawd, if I

didn't know the years had passed, I'd think he *was* Sammy."

Zelda cradled Ailey's chin in her hand. "And I would've believed you too."

Ailey wobbled a bit as he was turned this way and that.

"You alright, child?" Nanna Truth held Ailey's shoulders, turning him to her.

Suddenly his legs became jelly and his head a spinning disco ball. Nanna Truth was the only thing holding him up. His bones felt like they'd time-traveled somewhere else without him.

"Maybe you oughta sit down." Nanna Truth nearly carried him to the table and eased him into a chair.

"He almost got roughed up tonight," Taps said. "And hit by a truck."

"*Whaaat?*" said Nanna Truth. "Lawd have mercy."

"That's why I brought him with me. He wasn't sayin' much after it all and I don't know where he lives."

"You done right." Nanna Truth nodded. She pressed the back of her hand against Ailey's forehead and cheeks like his mom always did when he groaned that he couldn't go to school.

"Well, he don't feel too bad, only got a little heat to him." Nanna Truth bent down to be eye-level with Ailey. The hand towel draped over her shoulder swung forward as she tugged on it. "You're gonna be fine, suga. Just rest here."

She patted his thigh and headed to the kitchen. "A spoonful of cod liver oil will set you right."

Ailey's eyes grew big and so did Taps's.

Bottles clanked and cabinet doors *kreeed* opened and slammed closed.

Nanna Truth came back into the room with a light brown bottle, a glass full of cloudy liquid, and the largest metal spoon Ailey had ever seen.

Taps slid to a stop right by Nanna Truth. "He said he don't think he needs any cod liver oil."

"Now get back, boy," she said swatting Taps out of the way, laughing. "He said no such thing. This'll make you feel right as rain, babe."

The light amber liquid crawled out of the bottle and slithered into the curve of the spoon. If Ailey wasn't sick before, he sure was sick now. As if in slow motion, he watched her bring the ginormous spoon to his lips.

He squeezed his eyes shut and almost stopped breathing when the cold metal pushed against his mouth.

"This'll cure whatever's ailin' you, child." Nanna Truth tilted the spoon up, and with a bit of force shoved it between Ailey's lips. The spoon clinked against his teeth.

She might've been able to cram the spoon against his tongue, but Ailey refused to swallow. As the liquid crammed his mouth, footsteps slowed outside the front door.

"That'll be Sammy and Asa," she said. "I can't wait for Sammy to meet his twin."

At the thought of meeting his Uncle Sammy as a young man and his great-grampa Asa, Ailey swallowed, forgetting all about the cod liver oil hunkering down in his mouth. He gagged, nearly choking. He pitched forward in the chair as a tall dark-skinned man in a black suit, tie, and hat strolled into the front hall of the apartment. Through Ailey's tears and hacking, and Nanna Truth's thumps against his back, he could hardly recognize the young, lean Uncle Sammy behind him.

"What's happenin' here?" Sammy asked, as the older man closed the door, taking off his hat.

"This here's Ailey," Nanna Truth said. "He isn't feeling all too good at the moment. But I do declare, if he wasn't lookin' so green, he could be you."

"Be me?" Sammy came closer, studying Ailey's face. "Could he be so lucky?"

Ailey coughed, lurching forward again. Nanna Truth's hand slapped high across his back as he sputtered and hacked. The cod liver oil tasted exactly how it looked, thick and oily.

"What happened to him? And who is he?" Sammy leaned over and kissed Nanna Truth, then Zelda.

"Sammy, stop with all the questions, and give the boy some air." She held out the glass to Ailey, but he didn't think he could swallow another thing.

Sammy grilled him with his good eye. He wasn't wearing

an eye patch yet. Ailey tried not to stare. He failed miserably.

Taps's father stepped into the room, breaking the tension. He nodded a greeting and placed his hat on a hook.

Ailey had always been told his great-grampa was a good man, but a man of few words, and Ailey hadn't heard one yet. With one hand, Asa unfastened the two gold buttons of his suit while reaching for the newspaper resting on a side table with the other. He squeezed Nanna Truth's shoulder as he headed around the dining table for a club chair in the living room. Zelda sat on the chair arm next to her husband and rubbed at his neck.

"Welcome, young man," he said, after giving Zelda a light kiss on her cheek. "If anyone can get you right, it's Momma."

Nanna Truth beamed, turning back to Ailey. "Now drink this down."

Ailey eyed the glass suspiciously.

"Come now," she said, thrusting it forward. "This here's my sweet tea lemonade. Squeezed the lemons just this morning."

As Ailey took the glass, Sammy asked Taps, "Where'd you find my shadow?"

"He's not from around here," Taps said.

"I figured. He seems like he just jumped into port."

"How would you know?" Zelda teased.

"I got an eye for these things." Sammy tapped at the

corner of his good eye. "He don't look like a city boy."

Ailey tilted the glass back, avoiding Sammy's gaze.

"That's it. Finish that up," Nanna Truth said, brushing Sammy away. "That there's got the right amount of sour and sweet to coat your insides. You think you could get a couple pieces of fish in you too?"

At that, Ailey's stomach groaned.

"All right now," she laughed. "I guess that's a yes."

Even though Ailey felt like his every move was watched under a microscope, relief filled him. Because for another moment, he wasn't getting turned back out onto the street—alone.

CHAPTER TWENTY-TWO

SO THE STORY GOES

Ailey tried to make himself as small as possible in the dining room chair. But it didn't work. All eyes were on him.

"We probably ought to call his mother, let her know where he is," Zelda said, kissing her husband again before she left his side. "We don't need her worrying."

"You right 'bout that," Nanna Truth said. "Your momma got a phone? Or do I need to send Benji and Sammy 'round to let her know you gonna dine with us tonight? Give you a little strength before you head on home?"

Ailey swallowed the last of the sweet tea lemonade, nearly choking again. *Call his mother!*

"Yes, she has a phone," he whispered. "But she, um, might not be home."

"Maybe your father's there?" Zelda asked, resting her hands on the back of another dining room chair.

155

"I don't think he wants us calling his pops," Taps said, rushing to Ailey's side.

"Well then, why don't you at least try and call her? The phone's over there. I'd feel better." Zelda pointed to a black phone with a spinning dial. The kind Ailey had only seen in old movies and at museums.

Ailey wandered to the phone like it might bite. Then lifted the receiver. He felt everyone watching and listening. Nestling the phone against his ear, he heard someone laugh on the line. "I think somebody's using it," he said, relieved. He was about to place the phone back in its cradle when Zelda took it from his hand, stilling his shoulder with her other.

"This is what you get when you got a whole bunch of chatty neighbors sharin' the line. It's probably Edwina Evelyn talking to her sister. Don't know where she finds the money to keep yappin' on like she does." She pursed her lips and shook her head as she put the phone to her ear. "Evening, Salt. This is Zelda. Yes, I'm fine, thank you. But we need the line for a quick call. Emergency. Yes, yes, everyone's fine." Zelda rolled her eyes up to the ceiling, still nodding. "It'll be real quick. Hi there, Pepper, sorry to disturb your call."

When she handed the phone back to Ailey, there was silence on the other end.

"You best hurry," Zelda said. "Edwina is going to hold me to that minute."

Ailey turned back to the phone and let his finger swing around in the holes, picking random numbers. The phone made a funny zipping sound every time he rotated the dial.

"Hello?" he said when a voice came over the line. Everyone except Asa, who, tucked behind a paper, watched him. "Hi, Mom, it's me."

"I think you got the wrong number," the voice said. "You better reconnect with the operator."

"Yes, I'm fine. I'm at a friend's house . . . Taps, I mean Benjamin Truth," Ailey said glancing at Taps. "I wasn't feeling so well, and they've asked me to stay for dinner. Oh, I can? Yes, I'm feeling better."

"I told you, this isn't your momma, boy. Now get off this line!"

"I love you too, Mom. Thanks. I will. Bye." Ailey placed the phone back in its cradle. As he turned away from it, he knew they'd all been listening. Even though Zelda fussed with the curls of Taps's short Afro, and Nanna Truth folded napkins on the table, their eyes were on him. Sammy leaned against the living room door frame. "She said to thank you for having me." Ailey couldn't meet anyone's eyes, but he felt Sammy's one good one studying him.

"Well, that's settled then," Nanna Truth said, smoothing down the front of her dress. "Everybody wash up and come on before the food gets cold."

"Oh yeah, I forgot," Taps said, as his father folded his

paper and laid it on the chair when he got up. "You'll never guess who came tappin' with me today."

With everything that had happened, even Ailey had forgotten about the tapping.

"Who, li'l bro?" Sammy flicked Taps's ear. "Joe Louis?"

"Better." Taps put up his fists, and Sammy sent a play jab his way.

"Who could be better than the Brown Bomber?"

"Mr. 'Bojangles' Robinson, that's who." Taps crossed his arms, proud.

"The Mayor?" Sammy asked. "Get out of town! You tapped with the Mayor?"

"Yep." Taps nodded his head.

"Well, I'll be," said Nanna Truth. She and Zelda both smothered Taps in a hug at once. "Ain't that something . . ." She beamed. "Not that I'm surprised."

"Me either," Sammy said. "All us Truths got talent." He shadowboxed at the air, nudging Taps to battle him some more when they released him. "You showed him somethin', didn't you?"

Taps glanced over at Ailey. "He was there. He saw it."

Suddenly everyone's attention was back on Ailey, but this time, he didn't mind. He wanted them all to know how amazing Taps had been, especially Taps himself.

"He was great. The crowd was cheering and everything," Ailey said. His excitement was contagious. The Truths all seemed to lean in as they listened. "He flapped around like a bird about to take off." Ailey put his arms out and batted his hands through the air, hopping. "Then Taps went real calm and slow. Like he was walking. But there was so much clapping coming from his feet and the crowd. Then he kicked up his legs again and it was on. Bojangles could hardly keep up." Ailey mimicked Taps's dance moves the best he could, forgetting his own uneasiness. He even broke into a rap.

All eyes were on him
And Taps was the star
Even Bo said, "he got this y'all"
Taps tapped his feet to the sound of the beat,
Every move was tight, every move was sweet
Go 'head, son, I'll move how you do
Tap-pa-tap-tap
I'll do what you do
Tonight's your night
I'll shine in the back, 'cause you're shinin' so bright.
Pa-tap-a-tap-tap, I need to drop the mic.

Ailey let his hand spring open, pretending to let an imaginary microphone fall to the ground. As he slid to a stop, the floor creaked under his feet. It was the only sound. Everyone stared. At first, with pinched faces, then they broke into smiles.

"I'm not sure what all that was, but I like it!" Nanna Truth said. "Get it now." She snitched up her skirt and did a little dance of her own.

"Way to go, li'l bro." Sammy knocked Taps with a gentle right hook. Taps jabbed back. His smile was wider than the ocean. Then Sammy turned to Ailey. "You a poet or something?"

"Something like that." Ailey grinned, a bit out of breath.

"You're not bad either. But with a face like yours, I'd expect nothing less."

Happiness was going to burst from Ailey's chest.

"Okay, okay, let's carry this to the table. You know how I hate cold food," Nanna Truth said, pulling Taps in for another huge hug. "My grandson tappin' with the Mayor . . ."

When she came out of the kitchen, she placed a dish of cabbage and a bowl of corn in the center of the table. "Come on and sit." She tapped a seat back, motioning for Ailey. "Sit close to me, 'cause I wanna hear more about my sweet pea and the Mayor."

Ailey inhaled the spices as Zelda placed a platter of fish in front of him as he settled into the offered chair. Even though he kept catching Sammy's eye on him, Ailey hadn't felt this happy since he'd gone to the planetarium for a classmate's sleepover. But even that didn't top this.

This was family.

CHAPTER TWENTY-THREE

IS THAT WHAT NEWTON'S THIRD LAW MEANT?

The best nights were ones like these, Ailey thought. The night was clear. The sky speckled with stars.

"You want to practice some more?" Taps asked Ailey, as they sat out on the fire escape, skygazing.

"Sure, why not?" Ailey leaned back, searching the sky. He exhaled. Everything looked so familiar. Like Grampa had said it would.

Although the Harlem sky wasn't as clear as the skies over Upper Darby, Ailey saw stars. He'd spotted Polaris—the Guiding Star, the Drinking Gourd—but more importantly, he'd found Aida's Star. However, it didn't twinkle as brightly as it had in Upper Darby, when he'd made his wish and wound up in 1939. But it didn't matter. Right then he didn't want to make any wishes. He was right where he wanted to be: with Grampa.

"I figure this is as good a place as any to practice." Taps

hopped up. "And that rap you just did was something else. It could go real good with my taps."

"Works for me. But I could probably come up with something *even sweeter.*" Ailey grinned, mining his brain for a line that sparkled. "I'mma spit a fresh rhyme, poppin' like Nanna Truth's fish."

Taps's shoe clicked against the metal of the fire escape. *Clinc-clinc, clinc-clinc.*

The night sky so bright and freckled with stars . . .
Clic-clic, clic-cloc, clic-clic.
It's time to show Harlem who we are.
Clic-clac, clic-clac, clic-clac, clic-clic.
My heels click once
Clic.
My heels click twice
Clic-clic.
One more click, it'll spark the night.

"That's blip," Taps said.

"Blip?"

"Yeah, *blip.* It means it was good. It's slick."

"Thanks. I bet you can do it too. It's easy," Ailey said.

"It doesn't sound all that easy to me, throwing words together like that from nowhere."

"Give it a try and see. Isn't that what you told me?" Ailey

crossed his arms and stuck out his chin, smirking.

"You right." Taps nodded. "Lay it on me."

Ailey rubbed his hand together as if warming them in front of a fire. "Okay, first, get something in your mind you want to rhyme about."

Taps chuckled. "That's easy. The stars and tappin'."

"Works for me." Ailey studied the sky. "Here's your first line: *Lookin' at the stars—*"

"*Wishin' one was here,*" Taps added.

"*Watchin' my tappin' . . .*" Ailey put out his hand for Taps to give him the rest of the line.

"*Watchin' my tappin' with the sound in her ear.*"

"Nice." Ailey smiled, bopping his head. He knew Taps was referring to Aida but didn't let on. "*Lovin' life on this beautiful night—*"

"*This is my chance to make it all right,*" Taps ended.

"Not bad," Ailey said.

"It was all right. Now let's get your feet moving like that to the lines of your monologue. Soon, no one will question that you're a star." Taps nudged Ailey's shoe, staring at it a second longer than Ailey felt comfortable. "Funny, your taps look just like the ones Mr. Robinson gave me, only smaller."

Ailey squirmed when Taps kept looking at his feet.

"Where'd you say you got them again?"

"That you out there, Benjamin?" Two long black braids dangled out the open window directly above them before a dark brown–skinned girl poked her head out. Ailey's savior.

"Of course!" Taps's face lit up in a way it hadn't all day. Shining like when Ailey's dad had given Grampa the picture of Gramma.

"You and them stars." The girl glanced up, then looked back down again. "Who you got with you?"

"Come down and see." Playfulness bounced in Taps's words, a smile plastered across his lips.

"I can't," she whispered. She turned her back to them and sat on the window ledge, then swung her leg outside. "Momma thinks I'm just getting more thread." But as she spoke, she whipped her other leg out the window and stared down at them through the iron rungs of the fire escape.

"I'm Franny," she called out.

"Franny?" Ailey repeated in disbelief. Here he was, staring up at the girl who would one day be Gramma Franny.

"Yep, that's what I said." She narrowed her eyes at him. "Who you?"

"Ailey. Nice to meet—"

"Guess what?" Franny said, cutting him off, excited. She came down the stairs holding a small piece of fabric in her hand. A needle hung from a light blue thread attached to it. "Miss Lowe asked Momma to go down to the Broadhurst for her tomorrow. And Momma said I could go, too, if I promised not to get in anybody's way. But since I never get in the way, it was an easy promise to make. Isn't that—"

"The Broadhurst?" Ailey turned to Taps. He knew he should zip his lip, but he could never keep the zipper closed for long. "Isn't that the place you're supposed to go?"

If looks could slice a person in two, Ailey would have been diced after the look Taps threw his way.

"What are you going to be doing over there?" Franny asked. She pushed the needle through the corner of the fabric, pulling tight. "You thinking about becoming a sweeper or handing out programs or something?"

Taps stared straight ahead. "Yeah, I was thinking about it."

Sweeping? Why wasn't he telling her? She was going to be Ailey's gramma. *Why didn't he want her to know?* This time, even though he wanted to upchuck all Taps's secrets, Ailey kept his mouth shut.

"You know how that King boy is always bull-skating about going in there? Like he owns things?" Franny pierced swatches of cream and turquoise fabric with the needle while staring at Taps, who was gnawing at the inside of his cheek. "Well, I hope he's there tomorrow. 'Cause he's always promising to bring me over and introduce me to all the stars. Imagine knowing all those famous folks?" She rested her chin in the palm of her hand and dazed off.

Wait! What? Why wasn't Taps talking and why was she talking about King? She was supposed to be *his* gramma.

Even Ailey, who didn't have time to think about girls, knew Taps wasn't going to win her over like that! And he had to, otherwise Ailey could say bye-bye life!

"Taps is better than King will ever be." Ailey unzipped his lip. A lightning-quick jab from Taps's elbow met his side. "Ouch!"

"You don't have to tell me he's amazing. I know that." Franny stopped stitching.

Ailey was sure he'd heard a little salt behind her words. It was the same tone Jojo got when she wanted to make it clear she wasn't dumb, and no one was telling her something she hadn't known first.

"But one thing doesn't have anything to do with the other," Franny said, arranging the fabric in bunches as she spoke. "King is always in the middle of everything. I wouldn't be surprised if we see his name in lights one day."

Ailey thought about how Bojangles had stopped King from getting in the *middle* of things when he was with Taps. "He could be before King is." Ailey pointed at Taps, not daring to face him. He did take a side step out of reach of any other possible sneak-jabs though.

Taps let out a tight-lipped huff.

"King told me once that maybe one day he'd introduce me to the Mayor, because King's cousin is part of the show. Imagine . . ." Her voice was airy and light as if she dreamed.

"Taps could—" Ailey doubled over as Taps's fist connected with his stomach. A few steps away wasn't enough.

"Benji! What are you doing?" she asked, not missing his Superman-speed punch.

Even if Ailey wanted to speak, his breath was gone.

"I was teaching him about boxing," Taps said.

"Yeah," Ailey coughed. "The surprise attack."

As if she had a Benji Lie Detector, she watched him for a second. Then she remembered her excitement. "Not that I'm happy Miss Lowe broke her wrist," Franny went on. She pulled a pale pink square of fabric with curved edges out of her pocket. "But is it awful I want it to take a little time to heal?" She waited for them to answer. Ailey didn't dare. "She asked Momma to step in. Doesn't want someone taking her job. She knows she can trust Momma to do right by her." She looked between Taps and Ailey, folding and tucking the fabric in her hands. "She just got off the phone with Momma a bit ago. Some boy ran into her and her friends, tossing them off their feet, and then a man chasing after him knocked her down again. She landed on her wrist kinda funny. Broke in two places, I think." Franny shook out her hand as if she could feel the woman's pain.

Ailey's eyes bulged and his mouth dropped open. She was talking about him and Bumpy. He glanced at Taps and could tell he knew it too.

"You okay there?" Franny asked.

"Git your tail back in here, young lady!" a stern voice called from above before Ailey could think of what to say.

A woman about his mom's age, with freckled, light brown skin, leaned out the same upstairs window Franny had scurried out of. "What do I gotta do to keep you off this fire escape and behind that sewing machine?" She shook her head. "Evenin' there, Benji. Tell Sister Truth and Zelda I might be down a bit later to do a little needlework and listen to our show on the radio."

"Evening, Missus Criss." Taps gave a wave. "I will, ma'am."

"Gotta run," Franny whispered. "But I'll tell you all about the Mayor when I meet him." She giggled, and as she stood, the fabric fell from her lap.

"Wait, you dropped this." When Ailey held out the fabric, he realized she'd stitched an intricate flower with overlapping turquoise, cream, and pale pink petals.

Franny turned, her hand on the rail. "Keep it. Give it to someone you're sweet on."

"*Eeww*, I'm not *sweet* on anybody." Ailey scrunched his face like he could taste that cod liver oil again.

"Then give it to someone who might like it. Say it was made special for them. Girls always like that—feeling special." She fluttered her eyelashes at Taps, who didn't seem to notice. Then she raced up the fire escape and was gone as quickly as she'd come.

Silence stretched between Ailey and Taps. Ailey knew he'd put his foot in it, but he couldn't keep quiet. Franny was braggin' on King not Taps.

As he sat with his thoughts, Ailey slowly realized it was all his fault. Everything. His presence, the shoes, the stupid pocket watch.

If he hadn't traveled back in time, there wouldn't have been a chase, and he wouldn't now be worrying about Franny and King arm and arm. It was one more reason Ailey needed to get Taps up on that stage. And quick!

CHAPTER TWENTY-FOUR

FRANNY AND KING SITTING IN A TREE

Ailey and Taps sat in silence for a while after Franny left. Low, city rumblings the only sounds as they skygazed. Actually, Taps skygazed while Ailey tried to think, still holding the intricate handmade flower in his palm. His only thought—getting Taps to that theater. Not just so Bojangles could see him, but so Franny could too.

"Why don't you want Franny to know about you and the Mayor?" Ailey asked. He glanced at Taps who studied the sky.

"What's there to know?" He continued looking up.

"Lots," Ailey said. "For one, he wants *you* to audition. Not sweep up or hand out programs."

"Hold on a minute." Taps's stare pierced Ailey. "Who said anything about an audition?"

"The Mayor."

"I think you got that wrong," Taps said. "He wants me

to come show him my moves and return the shoes. That's it. He was just being nice."

"I don't think so." Ailey shook his head. "Plus, King wouldn't have been so mad. You didn't see his face when Bojangles said it."

Taps looked from Ailey back up to the sky. "Who cares what King thinks. I told you, he's just a struttin' peacock."

"Exactly. And Franny likes his feathers! You can't just give up like this. You have to go."

"Who said I'm giving up?" Taps crinkled his brow. "There's nothing to give up on. I'm just taking him back his shoes."

"But, you won't," Ailey sighed, kicking his foot against the railing.

Bbburrraanng echoed through the night.

Taps cut him a sideways look. He didn't understand what Ailey already knew. *But how could Ailey convince him?*

Ailey had to try a different approach. "Franny really likes King, huh?"

"Who said." Taps went rigid. "She does not."

"You sure? She kept talking about him. *King this and King that.* When my sister, Jojo does that . . ." Ailey rolled his eyes. "Heart doodles on EVERYTHING come next."

Ailey could feel Taps's mind starting to work. It needed another jab though.

"You want King introducing her to the Mayor?" *Jab.* "She'd *never* forget that." *Jab. Jab.* "Think he'll put King in the show?" *Jab. Jab. Jab.*

"How am I supposed to know?" Taps snapped.

"Okay, okay." Ailey put up his hands in defense. "I'm just saying King is really good and doesn't seem scared of anything." *Sucker punch.*

"Who said anyone was scared?"

"No one," Ailey said knowing exactly how it felt to be called scared. "I was just making an observation. He's fearless. I think that's pretty cool. And that's probably why Franny thinks he's *moo-rrr-ee* than cool."

Taps squinted, as if trying to see a far-off star without binoculars. Then his head whipped around to Ailey. "What about you?"

"What about me?" Ailey asked.

"You won't try again to be that Scarecrow. 'Cause you think somebody is better. You the one sound scared to me."

Ailey took the punch. Then turned the other cheek steeling himself for more. "At least I tried," he half whispered.

"Did you really?"

Skygazing was over. And if Ailey didn't know any better, Taps had mastered the Ailey Lie Detector too.

"What does it matter now? My audition's over." Ailey

peered down at his feet. "It's not like I can go to my teacher and ask for another chance."

"How come?" Taps prodded.

"Because it doesn't work like that." Ailey thought about Grampa telling him the same thing.

Taps shook his head. "You're scared, that's how come." His tone was gruff.

"That's not fair and I'm not scared," Ailey began then stopped himself. He wasn't going to play this game. More lying wouldn't help. It was time to find some grit. "Okay, so maybe I am scared. At least I'm admitting it."

"You're only scared because you haven't practiced." Taps said.

"That's not the only reason. You haven't heard Mahalia."

"Whatever. That kinda competition don't matter." Taps brushed the excuse aside. "Sammy always says, *See you. You're your toughest competition.*"

"Huh?" Ailey didn't follow.

"It means if you don't do all *you* can, you're already beat. Who cares 'bout anyone else. Be better than yourself."

"Are *you* already beat?" Ailey asked. "You practice all the time." A truck thundered down the block.

"I'm not trying out for anything."

Ailey channeled Mr. Rock cocking his eyebrow up to meet his hairline.

"I already told you I'm gonna bring the shoes back." Taps hoisted himself up by the rail. "I'm tired, I'm going to bed." Too polite to say it, he watched Ailey like he was ready for him to leave.

The conversation was over before it even got started.

As Taps yanked the window higher, out of ideas, Ailey whispered, "Can I stay?"

The curtains swept through the opening, caught in the breeze. Taps turned back to Ailey. The skin between his eyebrows dimpled.

Ailey crossed his fingers behind his back and crossed his toes inside Bojangles's shoes. He knew the last thing Taps wanted was a sleepover with a stranger who'd called him chicken. Ailey wouldn't have wanted it either, but even worse were the words he was about to say. *But desperate times . . .*

"My mom's not going to be home 'til late. And I kind of don't want to be there—"

"With your dad?" Taps finished. His slight scowl lifting.

Ailey let the lie hang in the air. An asteroid-size boulder of shame tried to knock him down. His dad was one of the coolest guys he knew besides Grampa. He didn't deserve this lie.

Taps pulled back the curtain and crouched, letting Ailey climb inside first. After he closed the window, they stood in the narrow space between two twin beds before Taps moved past Ailey. "I'd have to ask Momma and Nanna Truth."

Ailey held his breath as Taps headed for the door. He felt like he'd swallowed another heaping spoonful of cod liver oil. But he'd rather swallow that right then than wind up on the street again, with no way home.

CHAPTER TWENTY-FIVE

IT DOESN'T GO DOWN ANY SMOOTHER WITH CAKE

Ailey nearly plowed a trail across Taps's bedroom carpet. Pacing back and forth. Waiting for the verdict. Could he stay or would he have to go?

"I'll get you some pajamas," Taps said, coming into the room. "Momma said it's okay. At first, she wasn't too sure, but then I told her about your pops." Taps did a drinking motion.

That plate of worms tossed in Ailey's belly. Ailey wanted to gag. His dad was the last person who'd be drunk or do anything to hurt him. And even though Great-Gramma and Nanna Truth would never have the chance to meet him, Ailey didn't want them thinking he was bad.

"You gotta call a neighbor though. Leave our number for your mom," Taps added. "Mine doesn't want her worrying." He pulled open a drawer, grabbing pajamas. "Take my bed. Sammy sleeps in here too. Don't want you getting stepped on in case he wakes in the middle of the night and forgets someone's down there. He's stomped me plenty of times when family's visiting. It's not fun."

"Thanks." The tension in Ailey's shoulders loosened and he dropped down on a quilt of dark and light blue fabric that resembled the sky.

"Here." Taps tossed pajamas at Ailey. So Ailey decided not to mention his Black Panther onesie. "That's mine." Taps gestured toward the other bed. The one facing the window. Ailey bounced up, not wanting to be caught on Sammy's bed. "You better call now, before Missus Evelyn ties up the line again. I just checked. All clear."

Ailey followed Taps out of the bedroom.

"I'll grab us some moo juice and another piece of cake," Taps whispered, nodding toward one of the closed doors in the hall. The familiar whir of sewing machines behind it.

Taps already clattered around in the kitchen when Ailey reached the dark living room. Great-Grampa Asa's newspaper lay neatly folded in the chair where he'd left it before heading out for another shift as a Pullman porter over at Grand Central. Ailey picked up the phone receiver and, sure enough, someone was on the line again.

"Sitting behind her, I'm sure you couldn't even see li'l Miss Reverend Lee in the pulpit."

"I'm tellin' you. It was big. Ostrich big. Head full of feathers," the other woman on the line said.

"You reach somebody?"

Ailey flinched then spun around. The phone cord wrapping around him.

"Hello? Is someone on this line?" One of the women said into the phone. Ailey quickly hung up.

When he turned back, Taps was balancing pound cake on two glasses of milk. He placed one on the doily by the phone. And as soon as his hand was free, he shoved cake into his mouth.

"Yeah." Ailey picked up his pound cake and took a giant bite. "Um, Mrs. Merriweather is going to leave her a note," he mumbled. Mouth full. Swallowing down his lie with pound cake.

"You better take the bathroom first. Once Sammy comes from boxing, it won't be free 'til next week! He makes kissy faces and googly-eyes at himself in the mirror for hours. It's disgusting." Taps rolled his eyes.

Not wanting to stand between Sammy and a mirror or anything else, Ailey shoveled the last bite of cake in his mouth.

When Taps took their empty glasses back to the kitchen to wash, Ailey hurried to the bedroom. There was no way he was going to let Taps see what he had on under his shirt and pants.

As he reached the bathroom, carrying the pillow-soft pajamas that smelled of lavender soap, the water stopped running in the kitchen faucet. Whistling and jingling of keys drifted inside from the outside stairwell. Then the entry door creaked open, Sammy's voice filling the space. Ailey bolted for the pitch-black bathroom.

"Ah, there's the star." Ailey heard the smile behind Sammy's words. "My li'l bro dancin' with the Mayor."

Ailey started to close the bathroom door just as Sammy and Taps came into view at the other end of the hall. Fists raised as they bobbed and weaved around each other pretending they were in the ring. Sammy snapped his finger, off to the side of Taps's head, and when Taps turned to look, Sammy whistled and slapped Taps's face playfully.

"Remember the element of surprise," Sammy said. "You always gotta have your dukes up. Ready. You never know when you'll be able to strike. To surprise 'em. You dig?" He brought his fist against Taps's ear in a slow motion punch Taps wasn't ready for. Then he pulled Taps in for a headlock hug.

Ailey pushed the bathroom door closed right before the sound of their footsteps came closer.

"I want to show you something," Taps said in a hushed voice near the closed door.

"Whatcha got?" Sammy asked.

Their footsteps kept going.

When they were out of earshot, Ailey searched the wall

for the light switch, flipping it on. He splashed water on his face and gargled toothpaste, running his finger over his teeth since he didn't have a toothbrush. When he bent down, he hesitated, staring at the magical taps.

"You got me into this," he said and reached to untie them. Then he stopped. *What if he couldn't get them to shrink back after taking them off? Then he'd be stuck. Really stuck*! Ignoring the plate of now overturned squirming worms in his stomach, he slipped his slacks off and climbed into the roomy pajama pants, pulling the striped blue shirt over his union suit.

Turning off the light, he unlatched the door. When he approached Taps's bedroom, a sliver of light came from inside, slicing through the darkened hallway. Ailey reached for the doorknob.

"Your friend sure is jittery," Sammy said. "Somethin' peculiar about him."

Taps yawned. "He's alright."

"How you know? You said you just met the cat. Didn't you also say he snatched somethin'?"

"*No—*" Taps lay on sheets he'd spread across the floor.

"You said the daddy-o in the zoot suit was screaming 'thief.'"

"I didn't say he *stole* anything though. I said he said the man's pocket watch fell or something." Taps pulled a knit blanket up around his waist. "He got caught in the man's watch chain, I think. He's no thief."

Ailey appreciated Taps sticking up for him, but he still wanted to push open the door and defend himself, but Sammy was just like Jojo. He would never believe Ailey unless he saw it himself.

"You don't know that," Sammy warned. "He might've been born with sticky fingers. It's real interesting him wanting to stay when you got these."

Ailey leaned forward, peeking through the crack. Sammy held up Bojangles's shoes.

"Heck, these are worth something, and he probably wants to get his grubby paws on 'em." Sammy placed Bojangles's shoes on his bed.

"He isn't like that, I told you," Taps said again.

Sammy pulled a pair of polished brown shoes with square side buckles out of a velvet bag.

The same velvet bag that had held the shoes on Ailey's feet.

"And I'm telling you, *you* don't know what he's like." He pushed the buckle shoes back under his bed and pointed at Bojangles's shoes. "You better mind these while he's around. Folks funny when it comes to famous people and their stuff." He brushed the velvet bag across the top of Bojangles's shoes then slipped the shoes inside it. With his back to the door,

he pushed the velvet bag under his bed, placing Taps's burlap sack in front of it.

"*Mmmhmmm*," Taps sighed, folding his pillow in half.

"Don't *mmhmmm* me. But I'll tell you this, if you aren't going to watch him, I will." Sammy pivoted, still crouching. He pointed his finger toward his own face. "I may have only one workin' eye, but I'll sure be hawkin' 'til you audition for the man and bring them back. So, when you going? Tomorrow?"

"Come on." Taps punched his pillow with his head. "Not you too. I'll go when I go."

"Why not tomorrow? Or Monday bright and early?" Sammy added. "Don't want him forgettin' your face." Sammy got up and stood in front of the dresser mirror admiring his own. "Don't let no time pass on this, li'l bro. You can't let dust settle."

"I won't." Taps stifled a yawn.

"*Mmmhmmm*," Sammy said. The eyebrow over his good eye raised as he watched his brother from the mirror.

Outside the door, the floorboard under Ailey's foot groaned. All went quiet in the room.

The last thing Ailey wanted was to push open the door and step inside the light after being called a thief. But . . .

Kreeen . . .

That is exactly what he did.

CHAPTER TWENTY-SIX

THAT'S WHAT YOU GET, MESSIN' WITH THE WRONG COOKIE JAR

Taps rolled, half asleep, to look up at Ailey from the floor. "You get trapped in there?"

"Yeah, thought you fell in the toilet," Sammy added. He dipped his finger in a jar of hair grease and rubbed it between his palms. Then he swept it through his hair and glided a hairbrush down the back of his head.

Uncle Sammy was definitely a man of his word. Ailey didn't dare think what he'd be like if he'd had two good eyes, the way he already tracked him from the mirror as he crossed the room.

Ailey held his clothes against his chest. A shield. The tap shoes clanked against the wood floor. Then the rug muffled their sound. "Just washing my face." He finally answered when it was clear Sammy wasn't going to look away.

"Ah, and what a face it is," Sammy said. "Not as pretty as mine, but I have to say you *stole* a couple of my better features." He glanced at his brother, then continued checking himself out in the mirror.

Ailey's belly worms squiggled.

Taps's eyes were closed as Ailey stepped over his blanket tail and dropped the clothes at the end of Taps's bed. When Ailey pulled back the covers, about to climb in, Taps spoke.

"I know you aren't sleeping in those?" Taps opened one eye. "I love my taps, too, but not enough to sleep in 'em."

Ailey's knee hung over the mattress and his hand rested on the sheet. He wished he could dive into the blue of the quilt. "Course not." He tried to laugh but it came out more like a snort. "Just about to . . . um . . . take them off, wanted to sit first."

He sat on the edge of the bed. The quilt and sheets cradled his lower back. His fingers touched one of the intricate knots, and gave a gentle tug. It wouldn't budge. He didn't try again though. He didn't want to risk them popping back to regular size, or worse, for him to probably lose his way home if he couldn't get them to fit again.

When Taps turned on his side, fluffing his pillow, Ailey crept under the covers—tap shoes and all. He held his breath, closing his eyes. But a second later he opened them to find Sammy staring from the dresser mirror. The brush, hovering mid-stroke in his hand. Ailey's cheek pressed back in an awkward half-smile. He sank deep into the pillow

and yanked the quilt over his nose. When he peeked again, Sammy still watched his reflection in the mirror. There was nothing Ailey could do about it though. Sammy would just have to think him strange.

Sammy gawked at himself in the mirror forever. Not that Ailey could even sleep, but he didn't turn the overhead light off for almost an hour. Ailey had never seen a man "primp," as Grampa called it, for so long.

When Sammy finally switched off the light, it took Ailey a few seconds to adjust to the dark. Sammy's mattress squeaked and whined as he tossed and fidgeted.

Ailey rolled toward the wall where he could just make out newspaper clippings and black and white photographs pinned to it. In a couple images, two boxers held up their fists ready to fight. Underneath each image was a name: Henry Armstrong and Jack Johnson. Tacked up next to them were newspaper clippings of Joe Louis's latest fights. Ailey knew about some of them. After all, one of Grampa's favorite pastimes, besides bragging about Sammy, was reminiscing about the Brown Bomber or smiling about Josephine Baker, Jojo's namesake, and sometimes the Harlem Rens, his favorite basketball team.

There were even a couple articles and flyers showing

Uncle Sammy in the ring, or mentioning his KOs in bold black type. But closest to Ailey was a crumpled, then flattened, *Playbill* of Bojangles Robinson smiling in a marching band outfit with ornate shoulder pads above the words "*The Hot Mikado* Broadhurst Theatre."

Ailey stared at it, picturing Taps alongside Bojangles in a similar outfit. He knew Taps could be awesome. He just needed to find a way to get him to believe it too. But how? He couldn't even do it for himself. Suddenly he wanted to see the other tap shoes. Maybe they held the answer. Maybe they held a smidgen of magic too. Ailey knew it was a long shot, but maybe, just maybe, they could help.

He leaned forward in bed. Starlight and the moon blanketed the room in a soft bluish glow.

"Taps, you awake?" Ailey whispered. His own pulse thumped in his ears.

Kaaahhhzzz . . . kaaahhhzzz, was Tap's only reply. Sammy grunted, then snored, tossing and turning like he was in the boxing ring.

Ailey shoved the covers back and slipped off the bed. He crept across the rug and crouched near Sammy. Maroon velvet peeked from behind Taps's burlap sack under the bed. Ailey got on his stomach, careful not to nudge Taps or wake a snoring Sammy.

He slithered underneath the bed and stretched for

the velvet. Grasping a handful of fluffy-soft fabric, he slid back out and kneeled, pulling the bag into his lap. As he drew open the drawstrings and reached inside, the moon's shine appeared to be more brilliant than before. The same excitement that had raced through him at Grampa's workbench sped through him now.

His fingers tingled as they pressed into the leather of the shoes, sliding them out.

"What are you doing?" Sammy said. His tone even, as if asking Ailey if he needed another blanket. Not like he'd just caught him with his hand in a very off limits cookie jar. "I knew something wasn't right with you."

Before Ailey could sputter a response, or even close the bag, Sammy sprung out of bed and ripped it from Ailey's hands. He held the velvet neck tightly, probably wishing it were Ailey's throat. He towered over Ailey, his one good eye piercing him.

"I suggest you get up and get out now," he ordered. If he could've breathed fire, he would've right then. Fear held a stronger grip on Ailey, keeping him rooted. "Think I'm lying?" Sammy said. "Get your stuff and go. And if I ever see you 'round my li'l brother again, I can't promise you'll be standing too long, if you catch my meaning."

"But I just—"

Sammy shook his head and pointed toward the door. On

wobbly legs, Ailey backpedaled nearly stepping on Taps's head, but he collided with the dresser instead. The metal jar of hair grease tittered at the edge. Then fell.

Clink.

Taps's upper body flipped up, the blanket plopped to his waist. He swiveled, squinting. "What was that?"

"Nothing," Sammy said. "Just this thief hoping somethin' would drop his way."

The moment Ailey saw Taps's expression when he recognized the velvet bag Sammy still choked in his hand, Ailey knew he wouldn't listen to his reason. No one in the Truth house would believe him now.

"Why?" Taps asked a second later. His focus on the bag, not Ailey.

"What you mean, *why*?" Sammy said, not giving Ailey room for an explanation. "You know why. He's a thief."

"I'm not!" Ailey found a little fight.

But it didn't matter. Taps was already lying down and had turned his back on Ailey.

"I think you should go," Taps said.

Ailey almost hadn't heard him and wished he hadn't. Taps pulled the cover up, disappearing beneath it.

Ailey didn't move. He had to make this right. He had to explain.

"I wasn't stealing. Honest," he said. "You wouldn't

believe me if I told you, but I just had to check. To see if they were—"

"What?" Sammy spat. "As valuable as you think they might be? You're comin' up on the wrong riff, Jack."

"Huh?" Ailey said, moving closer to Taps, then immediately backing up when Sammy stepped closer to him.

He looked down at Taps's back, but before he could say anything else, Sammy dropped the velvet bag on his bed, snatched Ailey's clothes off Taps's bed, and wrenched up Ailey's collar. "You think I'm foolin'? I told you to git, and so did my li'l brother."

Sammy almost lifted Ailey off the rug as he ushered him out the door. Taps never turned back around.

When Sammy got Ailey into the hallway, he dropped Ailey's clothes on the floor and let the collar of the pajamas go.

Ailey shook worse than the paint mixer at the hardware store. His fingers kept slipping off the pajama buttons.

"Keep 'em," Sammy hissed in the quiet of the house. "I just want you gone. And don't show your face 'round these streets again. You dig?"

"But I—"

Sammy yanked open the front door. He shoved Ailey and kicked his clothes across the wooden floor.

Ailey didn't know whether to scream out, cling to the door frame, refusing to go, or just be pushed down the hall like a pitiful rag doll, tap shoes clapping. Nothing he said would make sense. Or make things better. And even more crushing was the fact that Taps didn't want to hear anything he had to say. So Ailey let himself be bulldozed out of the apartment.

The clothes smacked against the back of his head and fell.

Air rushed forward.

Whoosh.

The door shut.

The door locked.

Click.

Ailey was alone again in Harlem.

CHAPTER TWENTY-SEVEN

WHO SAID ANYTHING ABOUT A SWAP MEET?

How did everything go so wrong? Ailey fumbled with the pajama buttons outside the Truths' front door. His hands shook, and tears tumbled down his cheeks. Looking in that bag had seemed like the best idea at the time. *It wasn't.*

Now he was stuck and had no clue what to do.

He wished he had a slip of paper and a pencil to write *I'm sorry. I'm sorry. I'm sorry. It isn't what you think—I promise.* But he didn't. He doubted Taps would care anyway. Not with Sammy screaming "thief." After peeling off the pajamas, he pulled his clothes back on over his union suit. Wishing he had the Black Panther's smarts right about then. But that wasn't happening either. He folded Taps's things and laid them by the door.

He looked back one last time. Then he climbed to the next landing and curled in the corner, hoping to remain out of sight 'til morning. There were no hiding places. He tucked

his legs against his chin as scratchy music sailed underneath a closed door, wrapping around him. Soon, sleep rubbed at his eyes. His head drooped. Then he blinked awake rapidly looking around, shifting at the slightest noise, before falling back to sleep.

"Wake up." Someone jostled Ailey's shoulder. "You can't be here."

"Mom?" Ailey asked. His eyes opened, webbed with sleep.

"I'm not your mom, son. Come on, get up." The man nudged Ailey's arm again. He wasn't rough, but forceful. "You can't sleep on these steps. This is a nice, clean building. No riffraff."

"But I don't have anywhere to go." Ailey's voice sounded as weak and hollow as he felt, realizing it hadn't all been a dream.

"Well, you can't stay here. Stand up. And git." The man thrust his burly arm forward, pointing down the steps, toward the front door.

Ailey rubbed his eyes, disoriented. Then he remembered. Night still blackened the sky outside the windows above them.

The man leaned low, close to Ailey's face. He smelled of cooking grease and tuna.

"Where can I go?" Ailey asked.

The man let out a heavy sigh, like his last stitch of energy was leaving him. "I don't know, but you can't stay here. I'm sorry."

Ailey slunk down the stairs, then pushed open the front door of the building, letting the cool April air slap against his face. His foot hovered outside the door.

"Go on now." The man stood, arms folded, on the first-floor landing. Ailey stepped out into the night.

As the streets slept, Ailey tried to retrace some of his steps from earlier, but quickly realized he had no clue where he was or where he was going. Every street corner and every building looked the same. He traipsed up one block and down another avoiding dark alleys, unlit stoops, and anyone trying to get too close.

"*Pssst, pssst.* Nice ground grippers, li'l man."

Ailey started when a man poked his long neck and tiny head out from a darkened doorway. He reminded Ailey of a weasel he'd seen on *Animal Planet.*

"Wanna trade?" The man knocked over a bottle that rolled toward Ailey as he slid his foot from the shadows into the light cast by a streetlight. His shoe was barely a shoe. The leather had come away from the sole and his toes stuck over the front as if they'd busted through the seams.

"No, I'm, ah, good," Ailey said, hurrying away from the doorway.

He kept glancing back to make sure the man hadn't

gotten up and followed him. Once his heart stopped slamming against his chest, he stopped. He couldn't just keep wandering. He had to find a place to stay out of sight 'til morning. He wanted home.

After traipsing a little longer, down what felt like an endless block, Ailey settled on some stairs leading to a basement door. Two hulking metal garbage cans and a short cement wall blocked anyone from seeing him. He made himself as small as he could and hugged his legs, rocking. He stared at the hands of his Black Panther watch, wishing they'd sweep around like they did when things were normal.

Gimme home.

Gimme sleep, he whispered, exhausted and scared.

I wanna lay in my own sheets
I wanna see light. I wanna see home.
Not afraid of the night, but it's got me all alone.
No friend in sight. Got away from a fight.
Please, oh, please, I just wanna go home to escape this night.

He clicked his heels together. Just in case.

Nothing happened.

His eyelids grew heavy. Rhymes floated through his head, but soon he was asleep again.

☆ ☆ ☆

Ailey stretched his legs out in front of him. Then tucked them close to his body. He just couldn't get comfortable. His hand scratched the air for his comforter, but he couldn't find it. When his fingers landed on a sheet instead, he pulled it closer around his neck. It crinkled, poking against his cheek, scratching his skin. It smelled a bit strange, but he didn't care. He wanted a little more sleep. Besides his mother wasn't calling him yet. He tried to burrow his head deep into his pillow, then went as stiff as a signpost. A rock hard, cold wall meet his face. Everything zapped back into his mind.

He wasn't in Upper Darby.

Although he knew with certainty it was true, he didn't want to open his eyes and confirm it. The clamor of people on the street above him and the growl of passing cars tumbled down to his ears. Chilled air poked at his face, bugging him to open his eyes.

He tried to ignore what he already knew. *Maybe if I go back to sleep, I'll wake up in a better dream.* It was chilly and he couldn't get into a tight enough ball. He tucked his feet closer, but something felt wrong.

Yes, he was still in Harlem.

And yes, Taps had kicked him out, never wanting to see him again.

And yes, Sammy would pummel him into lunch meat if he ever went back to their house. But that wasn't the worst of it.

No, not even close.

When Ailey cupped his hands around his feet to keep warm, his hands grazed the fabric of his Black Panther unionsuit and its toepads.

He squeezed just to be sure.

Bojangles's shoes were gone!

Ailey's eyelids flew open. His legs sprang out in front of him. He gawked at his feet. The shoes really were gone. He closed his eyes again, hoping. *Please let this be a bad dream. Please.*

When he pried them open again, the printed image of the Black Panther's boots on the footsies of his pajamas were the only things covering his feet.

But how?

Then he saw it. Pieces of dark brown shoelace decorated the ground like chocolate sprinkles. He picked one up and the string continued to unravel between his fingers. Someone had taken scissors or a knife to it. Then he saw the jagged edge of a broken bottle.

He'd been cut out of Bojangles's shoes!

The worms in his stomach were having a full-blown party. He was going to be sick.

Perched between the two garbage cans he'd thought shielded him from view were a pair of tattered brown shoes.

Ailey couldn't believe it. That weaselly looking man had stolen Bojangles's shoes!

How had he slept through it? He had probably lost his only way home. He didn't dare ask out loud, but he thought— *it can't get even worse, can it?*

In the wind, the basement door shuddered against its frame. The crumpled newspaper pages he'd thought were his bed sheets rustled against him. Ailey stared out from behind the garbage cans. He wanted to stay hidden away, but that would guarantee he'd never get home.

He got to his feet. The hard, cool cement pressed against his heels. A couple people strolled by, not noticing him as he pushed aside one of the cans. He couldn't stomach looking down at the shoes that had been left for him.

Before he could even think to find Taps, he had to find the shoes.

CHAPTER TWENTY-EIGHT

THERE WEREN'T ANY WEASELS IN OZ

Ailey had to find the weasel.

The first place he thought to look was the doorway where he'd seen him. *But where was that?* He tried to recall his steps as best he could, but the doom tumbling into the pit of his stomach with the worms told him the man would be long gone even if he could find it.

Grampa had been right. The shoes weren't bringing him any luck either.

Ailey searched up one street and down another. Strange glances shadowing him, people catching sight of his peculiar socked feet. He didn't have time to care.

After a number of certainties, Ailey was certain yet again. He'd found the weasel's lair. But he almost wished he hadn't.

There was no sign of the slippery man or Bojangles's shoes. Only the smashed half of an empty bottle lay exactly where Ailey's foot had been a bumper car for it earlier in the night.

He stared at the doorway as if hoping the weasel would materialize.

He didn't.

Once again Ailey had proven he would mess up everything if given a chance.

He crumpled to the sidewalk, not caring who saw, and cried.

Singing wafted out of a storefront church a few stoops down from where Ailey slumped to the ground. In the open window, women with fans and white gloves clapped and stomped to the beat of the song. Their church hats bopped and swayed while the men's booming voices shook the air, rattling Ailey.

He wiped his eyes, searching the street, unsure what to do next. He was going to be stuck in 1939 forever. *There has to be some way out of this*, he hoped, trying not to give up—again. But he was all out of ideas.

I was sent here for a reason, he told himself, determined. Something or someone thought he could do this, even if he wasn't so sure.

One thing he *was* sure of, though, he didn't want to spend another night outside in the city alone. He had to find Taps and explain. He looked toward the sky, knowing he wouldn't be able to see Aida's Star in daylight. But he hoped she could hear him. "I'm not giving up. Not on Grampa." Even if he had no way home (something he refused to think about), he could at least try to make this one part right. "I have to change this."

He didn't want to think about Grampa lying in a hospital that stank of old cafeteria food, mop water, and disinfectant, troubled by his regrets.

Ailey got up, determined to get something right. One thing he did know—125th Street and Eighth Avenue.

CHAPTER TWENTY-NINE

SPILLING TRUTH

Almost two hours later, his heart nearly catapulted through his chest. He recognized Taps's pageboy cap at the end of the block.

Ailey sprang off the stoop and sprinted toward him. When he got to Taps, he reached for him. Taps yanked his arm back when he realized Ailey was the one who grabbed for him. His expression slammed Ailey hard, as if the force of it could knock Ailey through a concrete wall.

Ailey couldn't even call it hurt that he saw in Taps's eyes. It was so much more.

"Are these what you want?" Taps swung his burlap sack toward Ailey, opening it, so the velvet bag inside was visible. People weaved around them on the sidewalk. "Sammy was right about you." Taps tried to push past Ailey, but Ailey held his ground.

"I wasn't trying to steal. Honest."

"Yeah, right!" Taps said. "Were you planning on tapping the night away, even though you don't tap?"

"No." Ailey's shoulders fell. "It wasn't like that."

"What was it like then?" Taps stopped, then tried to pass Ailey again. "You know what, never mind. I don't want to know. It's just gonna be another lie." He hitched his sack higher on his shoulder and charged forward, steamrolling past Ailey.

"No, it won't be." Ailey watched the back of Taps's cinnamon-colored tweed jacket as he mingled with the late morning crowd. "I wanna tell you, but you won't believe me."

Taps kept walking. He didn't look back.

Ailey felt lost, desperate, and crazed all at once. But he wasn't giving up. "Benjamin Gannibal Truth," he shouted. "You were born in Louisiana to Zelda and Asa Truth. But you moved to Harlem when you were five." The crowd jostled him as he marched toward Taps, keeping in earshot. "You love Josephine Baker."

"Who doesn't?" a passing stranger joked. "That Wren is a queen."

"And the Harlem Rens," Ailey continued. He didn't mention his love of Franny, not wanting to jinx that future (or get punched). As he spoke, Taps blurred with the crowd. Rushing forward, Ailey yelled, "Sammy's your only brother, but your baby sister, Aida, died when she was two and you were seven. And that's how you started skygazing."

Taps halted.

Ailey surged forward. "The nights she wouldn't stop

crying, your mom made you take her on your fire escape for air. At first you didn't like it. Afterward you did. You rocked her to sleep out there. Looking up at the stars. She heard all your dreams."

Taps swung around and stormed through the crowd. He poked Ailey in the chest, sending him back on his heels. "How you know 'bout Aida? Who told you all that?"

Ailey steadied himself. "You did."

Taps stared. His eyes, thin slits.

"You lyin'. I didn't tell you no such thing."

"You did," Ailey said taking a breath. *Here goes.* "But it was in the future."

"The what?"

"The future," Ailey said. "It hasn't happened yet. But you will tell me in like seventy years."

"What are you talking? Seventy years . . . You must think I'm a jive turkey or something?" Taps scoffed.

"No." Ailey rushed on. "You're Grampa."

"That again?" The edge to his voice softened, but switched to concern. "You really need to stop your foolish talk."

"It's not," Ailey said. "You *are* my grampa. I'm from the future."

"You aren't right in the head." Taps bounced his fingertip off his temple. "I'm nobody's gramps. And what past do you think this is?"

Ailey sighed. "Just give me ten minutes." He held up ten fingers. "And if you don't believe me, I'll go." Saying the last words was like a needle prick to his skin. "I promise." Ailey motioned away from the crowd.

"I'm going nowhere with you," said Taps.

"*Pleeeeasssse.*" Ailey must have looked pitiful, because after a few seconds, a gush of air left Taps's lips and he followed him to the stoop.

"Ten minutes," Taps said once they both settled on the cold steps. For the first time he looked down at Ailey's feet. "What happened to your shoes?"

Ailey wiggled his toes inside his footsies. "I guess that's the best place to start. With the shoes."

Taps glared at Ailey like Ailey was trying to sell him air.

This was it. Ailey wiped his sweaty palms on his pants legs. "In about seventy years you're going to ask me to take care of Bojangles's shoes for you. Polish them and stuff."

"Now I know you're lying. I won't still have these." He raised the strap of his sack.

"You will," Ailey said quietly. "You won't bring 'em back."

Taps opened his mouth to speak but Ailey kept talking. He didn't want to lose a second of his ten minutes.

"So, after you told me about them, it was a secret, you know. I wanted to see them and try them on. When I did, I started dancing around and looked out the window and found Aida's Star and started talking to it. Made a wish." The words tumbled out of Ailey.

"What wish?" Taps question darted out.

"To change your stars," Ailey said going on. He didn't give Taps a chance for another question. He had to get everything out. "Anyway, once I made the wish, all of a sudden the shoes started acting real strange. They shrank and brought me here. I didn't know what was happening. But when I got here, near 125th Street, I knew it was to find you. The shoes were bringing me to you. Then I realized it was the exact place and at the exact moment when you were going to meet the King of Tap. They were magic. The shoes are magic!"

"Come again?" Taps snorted. "Shoes aren't magic. Stop trying to pull my leg."

"I'm not pulling anything. I tried them. Made a wish on Aida's Star. And here I am."

"You joshin'. Why that wish bring you here?"

"I guess because it was the start of your regret."

"My regret? What regret I got?"

Taps stared at Ailey and Ailey stared back.

"Not getting up on the stage."

"What are you going on about?"

"Bojangles," Ailey sighed.

Taps sucked air through his teeth. "Not that again. Told you, I'm going to go."

"No, you won't." Ailey didn't know how to get him to understand. "And it bothers you for the rest of your life."

"The *rest* of my life? Why?" Taps asked, as if he didn't know what else to say.

Ailey shrugged. "I think because it reminds you that you didn't try. That you didn't believe in yourself enough. You don't go."

Taps stayed silent.

Ailey could tell he was starting to wonder if any of it was true. "Do you believe you can get on the stage and be awesome?" Ailey asked.

It was Taps's turn to shrug.

"If you don't . . ." Ailey paused. "You're not going to tap anymore. Or at least not when people are watching."

"Now I know you're fibbin'." Taps sniggered. "I would never give up tappin'. It's how I breathe." He moved his feet across the step. "Ain't no way."

CHAPTER THIRTY

TRUTH RINGS TRUE
ALL THE WAY TO YOUR TOES

Taps's eyes searched Ailey's face.

"It's true," Ailey said. "You gave it all up because of the shoes." Ailey hated this truth, but he knew it was the only one that might get Taps to believe.

Taps looked down at Ailey's feet again and shook his head like he started to believe but didn't want to. "Sammy told me not to trust you." He pushed off the steps, about to leave. Then he glanced back at Ailey, hurt filling his eyes. "Did you make up these lies and hide your shoes so you could get these?" He nodded toward the sack over his shoulder.

"No!" Ailey grabbed for his sleeve. "Wait."

Taps tugged his arm free. "You must think I fell off a turnip truck too."

"I don't," Ailey snapped, nervous. He was losing him. "I'm not trying to take anything. I just want to help. It's all true. Honest. One minute I was in the hardware store, the next I was here watching you and Bojangles."

Ailey pushed back his drooping sleeve and looked down at his Black Panther watch. "This hasn't worked since I got here." He knocked against the face. A tear dropped onto his hand. He sniffled, batting it away.

Taps's gaze fell on the watch. Ailey rotated his wrist so Taps could get a better look.

"Who's this cat?" Taps ogled the watch face like he'd forgotten all about mistrusting Ailey and sat back down.

"The Black Panther. He's my favorite superhero. He's like Superman only better. You know Superman, right?"

"Yeah, course I do. His comic just came out."

"Well, Black Panther," Ailey added, "He's way better than Superman. Make Superman ten times more awesome and black, and that's him." He pointed to the watch, then unfastened it and held it out to Taps. "A lot of people don't know about him yet. Mostly just comic peeps. But one day Wakanda will be everything! I know it."

At first, Taps didn't take it, but curiosity won out. He studied the watch, his fingers running over the design. Then he pushed one of the buttons and the hologram spread over the sidewalk. The Black Panther crawled across the back of a man's shirt.

"Whoa!" Taps eyes bugged. "How'd it do that?" He started to turn the beam of light toward his eye, but Ailey pushed the button again, extinguishing it.

"Be careful. That thing can cause temporary blindness."

Taps held the watch out, cautious, but he didn't let it go. "What's the line on somethin' like this?" Taps asked, not taking his eyes off the watch.

"The line?"

He rubbed his fingertips together and looked over at Ailey. "How much it set you back?"

Ailey could tell he was trying to sound casual, but he wasn't doing a very good job. He chewed at the corner of his mouth like Ailey always did when he found something interesting.

"I don't know, maybe seventy-five dollars, maybe more."

"Seventy-five dollars?" Taps sputtered. "Now I know you lyin'. Where you get that kind of bread?"

"I didn't."

"I knew it." Taps nodded as if he'd finally caught Ailey in something.

Ailey hesitated. "You bought it for me. For my birthday. It's a limited edition."

"Here we go again." Taps's eyes rolled up. He thrust the watch back at Ailey.

"Flip it over," Ailey said, refusing to take it.

At first Taps did nothing. Then he turned it and read out loud. "My superhero. Love, Grampa."

"You gave it to me earlier this year. I wear it everywhere. It's my lucky charm."

The expression on Taps's face was a cross between seeing

a two-headed monster and hearing a person bark like a dog when they spoke, expecting you to understand.

"So, do you believe me now?" Ailey asked.

"This ain't no proof. Anyone could be your gramps. And I know it's not me."

"I get why you don't believe me." Ailey tried to refocus. "But I *am* from the future and you *are* my grampa!"

Taps dropped the watch into Ailey's lap when Ailey wouldn't take it. "That was a pretty cool trick with the watch, but I'm not believing any of what you're sellin'. I'm gone."

Ailey touched his sleeve again lightly to stop him. This time, Taps didn't pull away. "I don't know how it's possible, but it's true. Why would I make it up? How would I know about Aida's Star?"

Taps watched Ailey, not backing away anymore. After a few seconds he slid his burlap sack off his shoulder and pulled out the tap shoes.

Ailey had to admit nothing looked special about these either, kind of like before.

"So, you say they're magic?" Taps studied the shoes.

"I think so."

"Now you don't know?"

"Well the ones I had definitely were."

"And where's all that magic now?" Taps asked. "You know what, never mind. The less lies the better." He peered down at the shoes in his hand as if unsure of something. Then he glared directly at Ailey. He looked almost as serious as he did in the hospital in Ailey's time. "Promise me you won't run?"

"Huh?"

"Promise me?" he said more forcefully. "Sammy will think I'm the biggest icky on the block if you run."

"What are you talking about?"

"Show me." Taps thrust the shoes out to Ailey. "Show me the magic."

Ailey searched Taps's face, unbelieving. *Could it really be that easy? Could he prove everything to Taps and have a way back home?* He hesitated for only a second, then took the shoes out of Taps's hands.

People strolled by unaware how important this moment was for Ailey. For Taps.

CHAPTER THIRTY-ONE

WILL ABRACADABRA FLY IN HARLEM?

Ailey's stomach did flips. His hands trembled and his heart slammed his chest. The shoes were identical to the others. Every stitch and every crease was the same. Even the black mineral streak snaked along the sole of the left tap shoe. *This had to work.* They had to be magic too.

"Here goes."

Ailey slid into one shoe and then the other.

Again, his feet swam inside them.

Both Ailey and Taps watched his feet. Perfectly still. Waiting.

Nothing happened.

"I thought you said they shrank?"

"The others did."

"Well these aren't shrinking now." Taps leaned forward, squinting, as if making sure he hadn't missed something.

Ailey thought Taps might actually want them to be

magic. And so did he. "Maybe I need to dance. That's what I did last time."

"Okay . . ." Taps said, watching closely.

Ailey moved, a bit unsure, feeling foolish dancing on a busy street corner in Harlem. Grown man's shoes flopping on his feet as passersby eyed him strangely. *Welcome back to the circus.* Taps waited expectantly as if looking forward to the main event. Everything depended on Taps believing and the shoes shrinking. So Ailey could do his part to help.

Ailey took a deep breath and danced again, but something inside him already knew it wouldn't work. There was no night sky full of stars. And there was no Aida shining brightly to wish on. A few people slowed, probably thinking they were about to get a show, while others stopped, curious about an act that wore clown shoes. Ailey started to wish for the Black Hole again. He didn't want to think it, but he knew he was about to let Taps and Grampa down.

As if Taps sensed something was wrong, he waved his hands over his head. "There's nothing to see here. No one's performing."

Some people moved along, while others lingered like they thought Taps's announcement was part of the show.

Ailey knew he was running out of time—and hope. He didn't know what clock magic worked off of, but it was way too slow. He needed it now and wished everyone around them would disappear so he could concentrate. So, he could really dance. But they didn't stop looking and they didn't stop coming by. He had to ignore them. Remember why he was there. This was it. No time for him to be scared. He looked at the shoes, then over at Taps. Pity seeped into Taps's eyes. And that meant he didn't believe.

Ailey looked away, thinking of Grampa back home, and of Uncle Sammy talking about grit. Ailey had everything to lose if he didn't give this one more try. Remembering how Bojangles told Taps how to block out the noise and *turn off the radio,* Ailey focused, inhaling a deep breath. There were no visible stars above him, but that didn't mean Aida couldn't hear him if he wished hard enough.

Closing his eyes, he tuned everything out. Taps. The shoes. The people. Home.

At first, he heard the commotion of the city street, laughter, and distant conversations. Then a familiar melody played faintly in his ears, coaxed out of his memory as city sounds faded. He swayed. Words tumbling through his mind. His fingertips brushed against his pants, his arms swinging. His feet itched to move.

> *Can I win?*
> *Oh, can I win?*
> *Up at the top*

Far from the end.
Can I win?
Oh, can I win?

He bopped his head. And then he tried it again. Ailey was no longer on that street corner. It was just him and his rhyme and the beat bouncing through his feet.

It's Taps's time . . . It's Taps's time . . . Ailey chanted.
Come on, Bo's shoes,
don't fail me now
Taps needs to believe,
I can't let him down
He has to see the truth and magic
with Aida's Star,
to understand why I came this far
Today is the day for him to be great,
to tap with love and change his fate
We all may stumble,
and some may fall,
but a splash of courage can keep us tall
Come on Bo's shoes,
show Taps the truth,
let his fear fall away so he can be great
to tap with love and change his fate

☆ ☆ ☆

Ailey slid across the pavement. "*It's Taps's time . . . it's Taps's time . . . it's Taps's time,*" he whispered again, finding his breath. There was a split second of silence, then applause.

Ailey's eyes sprang open to find a small crowd of people surrounding him. Taking a minute to remember where he was and what he was doing, he scanned the brown faces for Taps. Hopping up and down to see over heads and around shoulders.

"Taps, Taps," he called. People tried to shake his hand or give him high fives and coins. "Taps?" he cried, whirling around, ignoring their smiles.

Grampa was gone.

Then as the people moved away, some *tsk*ing Ailey's rudeness, Ailey spotted Taps. He stood between a couple talking and laughing to themselves. Taps didn't laugh though. He stared at Ailey's feet. Ailey suddenly remembered what he had been trying to do. He looked down too. Then their eyes locked.

The shoes hadn't shrunk. The laces hadn't knotted. There wasn't any magic.

"You were alright, Jack." One man stepped in front of the invisible rope that had been connecting Taps and Ailey.

"Yeah, you were righteous, Slim," another man said,

lifting Ailey's limp hand to shake it. "Not understanding the shoe bit, but you were all right."

Another held out his palm like he wanted Ailey to slap it. "Gimme some skin, Jack. You really laid down that iron."

"Thanks," Ailey said halfheartedly, trying to reach Taps, who had turned to walk away.

"Here you go, li'l man." One of the men put a nickel in Ailey's palm. "Go get yourself some new ground grippers for your act. Then you'll really have somethin'." The men chuckled as Ailey nodded thanks, shuffling toward Taps. His feet sloshed against air in the shoes.

"Taps, wait."

"Why?" Taps didn't slow. "Sammy always says I need to keep a better eye, and he's right. I can't believe I actually wanted to believe you. There ain't no such thing as magic."

"But there is. What about Aida's Star?"

Ailey crashed into Taps when he whirled around. "What about it?"

"You said it twinkled brighter than you'd ever seen after she died. That was magic."

Taps bore down on Ailey, "Don't go using my baby sis. That wasn't magic. That was a big brother missing his baby sister and seeing what he wanted to see. That's not this." Taps turned to go, then stopped. "Give me back my shoes." He held out his hand as if just realizing that he was about to leave without them. The look crossing his eyes told Ailey that Taps wondered if this was Ailey's plan all along.

Ailey swallowed hard, not moving to take off the shoes. He had one more chance. "But they aren't really yours, are they? You promised to take them back. Were *you* lying?" He knew it was an unexpected jab. *But that was how you got your opponent, right? Sneak attack.*

Making Taps mad seemed the only option Ailey had left.

Taps balled his outstretched hand into a fist, then loosened it, pointing at Ailey. "Why you keep saying I'm not gonna bring them back? I am."

"You don't," Ailey stressed. "You never do. That's how I got them."

"Why wouldn't I keep my word?" Taps asked. "A man's word is all he's got."

Ailey was silent for a second. Then he said, "I know you don't want to admit it, but it's because you are scared."

He saw truth clearing Taps's eyes.

Taps believed this part of his story.

"You didn't think you were good enough," Ailey confessed. "But you are."

CHAPTER THIRTY-TWO

TOLD YOU, CHICKEN'S NOT MY NAME

"**Y**ou are," Ailey said again as a man's coat brushed his arm. "You *are* good enough."

Taps opened his mouth, then closed it. He didn't meet Ailey's gaze.

"It's okay. I'm scared too," Ailey admitted as the city buzzed around them. "But you can still bring Bojangles back his shoes. There's still time."

Silence pushed between them.

"What are you scared of?" Taps finally asked. "Out there, that was the *mezz*. I mean, you were great. Really great! Amazing actually."

Ailey was frustrated. Frustrated Taps kept throwing "being scared" back in his face. Frustrated the shoes hadn't done what they were supposed to do. And frustrated that he wasn't any closer to fulfilling his wish. But he didn't say that. This time, he knew better. "Same reasons as you maybe. But for me, I've never really given anything my all. Not like you. You put everything in your tappin'."

"You put everything in your raps. Or you have when I've seen 'em."

"Yeah, but when stuff's important, I find a way to mess it up."

"I don't believe that. You really gave a show out there." Taps glanced back toward the corner. "You still wanna be in that play you were telling me about, don't cha? Be that Scarecrow?"

"Yeah, but it's not that simple," Ailey said. "But who cares about that right now. We're not talking about me. This is about you and these." He pointed to the shoes still on his feet. "You have to bring them back. Find some *grit*, like Sammy says."

"How you know about that too?"

"I told you, I learned it in the future. Uncle Sammy said you were too busy shaking in your boots to find grit . . . Are you?"

Taps didn't answer.

"I could tell you that," King said.

Ailey bucked, startled. King always appeared when Ailey didn't want him to.

"Of course, he's yella . . . *bwok-bwok*." King strutted over to them, Zee at his side.

"Yeah, he's yellow." Zee tucked his hands under his

armpits and flapped his elbows like a chicken again; his camera banged against his shirt on a neck strap. "He knows he's gonna flop—*splunk*."

"Who asked you?" Ailey said.

"No one had to." King swiped his finger around the rim of his derby hat. "I was just tellin' it like I see it. He's not going anywhere near the Mayor 'cause he's chicken."

Ailey didn't stand as tall as the other boys, but it didn't matter. He got close to King's chest and gritted his teeth. "My grampa isn't afraid of anything."

King stared down at Ailey. Zee stopped clucking, and Taps closed his eyes in an extra-long blink.

"What you jabberin' about now?" King asked, looking around. "No one's talking 'bout your gramps."

Everyone's focus bore into Ailey.

He'd slipped up again, but it didn't matter. "Taps isn't scared of anything."

"Then prove it." King stuck out his chin. "I see he's given the Mayor's shoes to you. Are you going to take his place?" he smirked.

Ailey felt five years old, standing with fists clenched, on a street corner in a big man's shoes.

King chuckled and turned to Taps. "If you're not scared, do as Ducky here says and get up on that stage. Or is he a liar?"

The challenge whizzed through the air and splattered at Taps's feet.

King seemed to know a lot about Taps. Ailey ground his front teeth into his bottom lip and rocked, willing Taps to speak. But he didn't.

"See," King said and thrust his shoulder in Taps's direction. "He ain't got what it takes. I would've been on that stage the second the Mayor told me to come. Heck, I would have been waitin' there all black. Would've slept outside." King did an impromptu tap routine. "When you got a gift, you use it. Simple as that. Otherwise you spittin' in the face of who you got it from." His feet moved fast, but not as fast as Taps could. Before he'd finished, Taps had turned away.

"Come on, Zee, let's truck. These squares aren't gonna do anything worth seeing." Zee flapped his elbows again and waddled off the sidewalk after King.

Ailey joined Taps on a nearby stoop. The silence between them blocked out all other sound.

"Let's just go," Ailey said when it got too unbearable.

Taps's head had dropped, then he whispered, "Just give me back the shoes."

"Okay," Ailey said. Then his voice went shaky. "Um . . . but right now we have to go." Ailey turned Taps's head toward the man striding down the block in another funny looking suit that nearly swept the ground as he bent his knees, strutting.

At first Taps didn't seem to recognize him. Then he leapt up, grabbing his sack. "Snap, that zoot suit man."

"Quick. I don't think he's seen us yet," Ailey said and slipped into the cluster of people passing by.

They hustled away, Ailey doing his best in the oversize shoes. When Ailey peered back. Bumpy was too busy tipping his hat and grinning at passing women to notice them. But when Ailey turned back toward their escape route, he tripped where sidewalk battled a tree root and lost. He tumbled out of one of the shoes.

"You okay, baby?" A lady leaned forward to give him a hand. Taps helped too.

"Yes, I'm okay. Thank you," Ailey said as she continued down the road in Bumpy's direction. When Ailey picked up the shoe, looking up, Bumpy stared back at him. Recognition reaching his eyes.

"Eh, I know you two busters!" He squinted and pushed through the crowd. The coat of his royal blue zoot suit flapped as he moved. "No sense trying to run. I see you now. And I plan to finish what started last night. I don't never forget. And you leavin' me tangled with that copper, I won't definitely forget." He tapped the side of his head with his finger. "But too bad for you, he ain't 'round now," he smirked.

Ailey took one look at Taps and they both spun and ran.

"Shake a leg," Taps said. He bolted down the block, Ailey in his dust, half hopping, half running behind him. They dodged one gaggle of people and bounded around an army of boys playing leapfrog. Ailey was about to head into the street again, but Taps snatched him back. "No, this way."

"Go ahead," Ailey yelled. "I'm coming." He stopped and yanked off Bojangles's other shoe, grabbing it up. They were never going to get away if he kept stumbling over his own feet.

Bumpy was on their heels, even with Ailey out of the shoes.

Every time they thought they'd lost him, he kept on coming. Fist raised, yelling. Then, when they sped around a corner and Bumpy was out of sight for a split second, Ailey thought he knew better than Taps and cut right, ducking down an alleyway. Taps kept running straight. He had gotten far ahead of Ailey. Ailey was about to call him back, but didn't.

Bumpy would never be able to catch him. Taps was way too fast.

When Ailey realized, however, that he'd stupidly turned down a dead end, he tried to become part of the wall in a shallow doorway. He stood on tiptoes so his footsies wouldn't poke out. Right on time, too, because just like in the movies, Bumpy darted past his hiding spot.

Ailey exhaled.

But also like in the movies, Bumpy doubled back.

He came to a dead stop at the mouth of the alley and the doorway. There was nowhere left to hide or any way to get out besides the way Ailey had come.

And Taps was gone.

Slowly, Ailey inched along the wall, away from Bumpy. The bricks scratching his back. He hugged Bojangles's shoes to his chest as he crept deeper into a dead end. Ailey swallowed hard at the thought of—A. Dead. End.

"Leave me alone," he warned with more force than he felt. "I wasn't trying to steal your stupid watch."

"You think I care 'bout that? That watch ain't nothin! I got plenty more." This time he plucked up a silver watch chain attached to his pocket. "That copper almost pinched me. And Bumpy don't like getting pinched."

Ailey cowered. He held up his palm. His ill-fitting sleeve slipped down his arm, his watch exposed. Unfortunately, he didn't feel the strength of the Black Panther. He had no way out. He kept backing up. Trash crunched under his feet. Then solid brick, stretching wide and far above his head, stopped him.

Boxed in, there was no escape.

Bumpy was on him fast. His fingers snapped around the fabric of Ailey's shirt like a crocodile snatching a helpless bird. "Nobody makes Bumpy look like no chump."

Ailey swung his foot out, trying to kick. Bumpy bowed his legs.

"Uh-uh, not this time, Jack. You ain't gettin' me twice."

Ailey knew even if his foot met Bumpy's shin it'd probably hurt him worse without shoes. He squeezed Bojangles's shoes tight against his chest. Wishing that if they ever held magic, they'd make him disappear.

"What do we have here?" Bumpy said eyeing the shoes. "I bet I could get a pretty penny for these." With his free hand, he tried to pluck the shoes from Ailey.

"Leave him alone, Mister," Taps said over Bumpy's shoulder. "And don't touch those shoes. Someone's expecting them back."

Bumpy spun, smirking, releasing his hold on Ailey's shirt. "Well, well, well, what do we have here?" Ailey was still trapped behind his back. He mashed himself against the wall, trying to get out of Bumpy's reach. "And if I don't?"

"I'm warning you, Mister. Go about your business. I don't want to have to use these." Taps got in a boxer's stance, fists leveled in front of his chin, like Ailey had seen him and Sammy do the night before.

Bumpy let out a roar of laughter that poked Ailey's ears and bolted up his spine. "Whatcha gonna do with those?"

"Don't make me show you. Leave him be." Taps's voice

was almost a growl. His nostrils twitched, but no other part of him moved. "He's family. And you don't mess with my family if you don't want to mess with me."

Laughter continued to erupt from Bumpy's throat as Ailey's heart tightened. "I don't have time for this," Bumpy said looking between Ailey and Taps. "Give me those shoes, boy. I have a rep out here in these streets. You better recognize it, Jack."

"I told you," Taps shouted before Ailey could react. He moved into the mouth of the alley. "Don't touch him and don't touch those shoes!"

Bumpy took a step away from Ailey toward Taps, whose fists were still raised as he bounced on his toes. Ready.

No matter how ready, Bumpy loomed over Taps.

"Eh," Ailey called, trying to draw Bumpy's attention back. His voice trembled and so did his hands. He couldn't let Taps do it all alone. He pushed his sleeve back and pressed one of the buttons on his watch.

The Black Panther let out a low *Grrrr*. Bumpy's head flew back, cackles rocketed from his mouth.

Ahhh, shoot, shoot, shoot. Not that. Ailey scrambled for the other button.

The hologram of Ailey's favorite superhero spread out in front of him. He tilted his wrist, aiming the beam of light directly at Bumpy's face when he turned.

"*Ahh!*" Bumpy shrank back, blinking, trying to shield his eyes. He wasn't laughing anymore.

Ailey didn't waste a second. He cradled Bojangles's shoes tighter and took off, launching past Bumpy as Bumpy reached for him with one hand while he rubbed his eyes with his other. His fingertips grazed the fabric of Ailey's shirt but didn't take hold.

"Let's go!" Ailey raced toward Taps, whose fists were still up. He bounced from one foot to the other, ready if the flash of light wasn't enough.

Bumpy staggered, clawing for Ailey. "I'm gonna put a hurtin' on you, boy!"

Grampa and the directions were right. The watch *did* need that "may cause temporary blindness" warning label. Though Ailey didn't want to stick around to see if the *temporary* part was true.

Taps grabbed at Ailey's wrist as they reached the opening of the alley and the sunshine. He didn't let go. They took off as Bumpy hollered after them.

"This ain't finished!"

But Bumpy didn't wander out into the open.

Ailey wasn't sure where Taps was leading him, but he was sure, whether Taps liked it or not, he was going to stick to him like gum on the bottom of a shoe.

CHAPTER THIRTY-THREE

ALL IT TAKES IS A DOG NAMED KING

Ailey and Taps were almost out of breath as they dashed through the streets. Away from where they'd left Bumpy.

Yanking off his cap, Taps checked over his shoulder again, then slowed. "I think we lost him." His breaths, quick and shallow.

Ailey gripped a knee with one hand, hugging the shoes in the other. He took in large mouthfuls of air. "Wow, that was tough. You didn't even look scared," he said once he'd caught a breath. "I thought you were actually going to punch him."

"I was ready to."

"Did you mean what you said back there?" Ailey gulped down more air.

"What?" Taps asked. "About you being family?"

"Yeah, that, but the other part too. Did you mean the part about the shoes? That somebody needed them back?"

"You don't give up, do you?" Taps shook his head, wiping his sleeve across his brow. "You should try being this determined about playing the Scarecrow."

"Look who's talking," Ailey said, holding up his fists like Taps had against Bumpy. "You should try being fearless and go see the Mayor. Now!"

Taps settled his hat back on his head. "This again? Can't we talk about something else?"

"This is important. Why won't you just believe me?"

"Because you aren't provin' anything," Taps snapped. "Sammy always says don't believe someone telling you the sun's shining if you can't go outside and feel its heat."

"I don't know what else to say." Ailey admitted in frustration. "I've told you everything. So, either you believe me or you don't. But if you don't, explain how I know all these things about you when you never saw me before yesterday? Explain why my middle name is Benjamin and why you have a drooling dog named King?"

"I gotta dog named King?" Taps laughed. "I always wanted a bulldog."

"Yep, well you've got one," Ailey said.

"Really?" Taps beamed.

"He's fat and lazy and farts and drools."

"Sounds like another King I know, minus the fat part." Taps chuckled. "So, I have a dog . . ."

"Wait?!? Are you kidding me?" Ailey asked. "All I

needed to do was mention you have a farting bulldog and you would've believed me?"

Taps was silent longer than a trip to the center of the Milky Way and back. "I freeze up when people are watchin'," he mumbled a few seconds later, traipsing away from Ailey.

For a second, Ailey, confused by the flip in conversation, slowed. Then he rushed to catch up to Taps.

"Out here I start off alone." He shot Ailey a bashful look. "But when people are starin', I forget everything."

Ailey understood. "I know *exactly* what you mean. But I don't think anyone would believe me since I'm always clownin' in class. But when people start watching me for real, I totally forget everything. Poof! It's all wiped out of my mind. Is it like that for you? You start thinking all those people are watching because they want to see you fail?"

"Pretty much," Taps agreed. "It's awful. All my doubts start flooding my brain, and I just can't remember."

"It's awful—"

"Worse than awful."

"And the longer I stand frozen in front of everyone, the more I forget—" Ailey felt Taps watching him, though he didn't turn his way.

"And the more you doubt."

"I really did want to be that Scarecrow, but when all eyes were on me, and my classmates started laughing, I couldn't even remember how to dance, and I'm always dancing. It was like I never knew how. I wanted to crawl under the floor."

"Exactly," Taps said. "No sense in embarrassing myself like that, especially in front of the Mayor. I've entered competitions before and it's not fun to freeze on no stage. I can't even find my feet to run or my knees to crawl."

"Right." Ailey couldn't help but agree. "There's no point asking for another chance, if I'm going to look like a fool *and* get stomped by Mahalia's voice anyway."

"But you can make those raps," Taps said. "Can she do that? The one you just did in front of the crowd was a blip."

Ailey flicked his shoulder forward. "It was alright."

"It was more than alright, and I bet you could make it even better. Like you did last night. You just need to practice it. Besides, today you weren't nervous at all doing your rap in front of everyone."

"Yeah, I was." Ailey shook his head fast. "But getting you to believe was more important. And once I got started I was lost to everything but the beat in my ear and the rhyme."

"That's how I get." Taps stared up the street. The sun was shining down on them. "But you know, people were already peeping you when you started. I never can."

"That's not true. You did when Bo told you to just close your eyes and turn off the noise. The radio, remember? And that's what I did. I forgot everyone and everything around me and just fell into the beats I'd been hearing in my head for days. That Crow's Anthem song from the play." Ailey surveilled the street before sliding his iPod out of his pocket. He handed Taps the earbuds. "Put these in your ears."

Taps eyed the white, odd-shaped blobs like they were spoonfuls of cod liver oil, but he looped the cords over his ears.

"No, like this." Ailey unwound them and pushed them into Taps's ears, hitting play. Michael Jackson's voice rang out as the Scarecrow. Taps leapt, jolted by the music filling his head. He nearly yanked out the earbuds.

"Get out of town, Jack!" He shouted, not realizing the volume of his voice.

Ailey turned down the music. "If you like that," Ailey said tapping the screen of his Nano a couple times, "you'll love this." When the screen lit up with Michael's *Smooth Criminal* video, Taps was all teeth. He couldn't grab the iPod quick enough. His eyes big as Michael danced across the screen doing his famous lean. Then all of a sudden, his smile dropped.

"What happened? Make it do that again."

Ailey took the iPod. No buttons worked. The screen black. "Sorry," Ailey said. He hated seeing the disappointment in Taps eyes. "The battery died. It won't work anymore."

Ailey didn't try to explain about chargers, USB cables, battery life, or iTunes.

"Is it broken?" Taps sounded worried.

"No, it just doesn't have any more juice."

"Like when the power goes out?"

"Exactly."

"That was the coolest thing I've ever seen." Taps stared at Ailey for a second. "Do they have a lot of stuff like that in the future?"

Ailey smiled. "Tons."

"Cool," Taps said again, his eyes never leaving the bright orange Nano. "I can see how that can help you block everything out."

"Yeah," Ailey smirked. "We need to trick ourselves into believing we're alone."

"How you plan on doing that now?" Taps motioned toward the dead iPod.

Ailey wound the earbud cords around the Nano and stuffed it back in his pocket. "By closing my eyes and thinking about my raps."

Taps squinted, unsure. "You think that's gonna work?"

"Can't hurt to try," Ailey said. "Besides its better to try than have regrets, right?"

"Yeah. You right." Taps rocked his head. "Regret's nothin' nice."

"Hey," Ailey said. "That could be the beginning of a sweet rhyme."

"How?"

Ailey snapped his fingers and bounced on his toes.

"*Regrets, regrets/Regret's nothin' nice,*" he began. "*Check one, check two/On this stage, fear ain't got no room.*" He shifted his shoulders back and forth. "*See, this is my cue . . .*" Then he pointed to Taps to add a line.

"*To tap my feet . . .*" Taps said, looking up, thinking. "*And do what I do—*"

"*Right now, it's all on me to be all I can be,*" Ailey added. "*With one breath, and one step—*" He nodded, encouraging Taps to create another line.

"*This is my chance to do my best . . .*"

"*With Sammy's grit . . .*" Ailey held an imaginary microphone in front of Taps, like his dad always did.

"*And shinin' stars/It'll be easier in the end/Not as hard,*" Taps finished.

Ailey hopped up and down. The heels of Bojangles's shoes rubbed against his chest. "You got this! That was it. Soon I'll be calling you Mister Tap-T."

Taps smiled, joining in as Ailey repeated the lines to their new rap. Then he crossed his arms and watched Ailey with the focus of a cat right before it pounces on a mouse. "Maybe we oughta make a deal."

"Another one?" Ailey asked. Even though Taps seemed to have had a rush from making the rap, Ailey tightened his grip on the shoes, unsure of what Taps was about to say.

"Yeah another one," Taps replied. "I'm still sitting with all this future talk, mind you. But I was thinkin' I'll go see the Mayor—"

"Really?" Ailey cut in.

"Yeah, I'll go see the Mayor if you promise to ask for another try. No sense in us both regrettin'."

Ailey didn't hesitate. "Deal."

CHAPTER THIRTY-FOUR

WE'RE OFF TO SEE THE MAYOR, THE WONDERFUL MAYOR— OF HARLEM—NOT OZ

Got me runnin'
Got me shook
Almost caught on a hook.
Taps put up his dukes
At the moment of truth
Tappin' down the street
To the sound of a beat.
No doubt
No fear
His time is here.
I said, no doubt
No fear
His time is here.

Taps clapped and tapped, gesturing at Ailey's feet, encouraging him to keep tapping as he rapped. Ailey felt like a circus clown trying to do everything at once, especially in footsies. But he didn't care. Besides trying to rap, clap, and tap, he was aware of everyone who stared as they passed. But if Taps could ignore them, he could too. Taps's focus was on helping Ailey, and Ailey turned his to helping Taps.

"*Aah*, man," Ailey said, after nearly tripping. Taps wanted him to speed up his taps with the tempo of the rap. It wasn't happening.

"Try this," Taps said. "You gotta concentrate. It's a relaxed, easy beat, kinda like . . ." His foot did what looked like a slow lazy *pa-dap-dap-dap*. To Ailey, achieving that sound while standing still would have been a lot, but doing it while moving would have been nearly impossible for him, even *in* shoes. "Don't focus so hard," Taps said. "Let it come natural, like your raps. Soon you'll lose yourself in the steps, and can't nobody pull you out. Nobody. *Regrets, regrets. Regret's nothin' nice . . .*" Taps started again.

"*Check one, check two/On this stage, fear ain't got no room.*" Ailey fixed his eyes on Taps's feet. They glided across the sidewalk. *Kapac-kapac-ka-pac-pac-pac.*

"You're meant to be up on a stage," Ailey said.

"And so are you."

Ailey scratched his head. "Wish you could've told my feet that when I auditioned."

"*Pe-shh.*" Taps smacked the air with his hand. "Forget about that. You'll be ready next time. Besides, I know some things. I'm a Benjamin, remember? Named after a man who can see the stars. And I see one right in front of me."

"Well, I see 'em too." Ailey smirked. "You're not the only Benjamin 'round here." He gave Taps a goofy grin.

Taps chuckled, then broke eye contact, glancing into the street. "Follow me," he said.

When the traffic idled and the street was clear, they hurried across and ambled a few blocks in silence. As they meandered, a tiny part of Ailey hoped Taps wasn't backing out on their deal.

Then Taps pulled Ailey across the sidewalk.

"Come over here." Taps motioned Ailey forward. "Rub this."

"Huh?" Ailey stopped on the curb, his back to the busy intersection as Taps brushed his hands over an old tree stump. "What are you doing that for?" Ailey asked, looking around.

"It's the Tree of Hope. Everyone rubs it before a big audition or before just going on a stage. It's for luck. And after everything that's been happening, I think we need it, don't you?"

"Thought you didn't believe in luck?" Ailey said, thinking of Grampa and his watch.

Taps's hand swept back and forth across the stump. "Believing in a little something outside yourself can't be too bad."

Ailey copied him. "What happened to the rest of the tree? It doesn't seem so lucky."

"It got chopped down," Taps said. He stroked the stump one last time before moving away. "Had to make room for a wider street or some such thing. But the Mayor brought it to 131st and dedicated it to the people. All sorts of famous people showed up on the day he did it, too, even the white folks' mayor, Mayor LaGuardia. Mr. Bojangles can get the attention of anyone he wants."

"And he wants yours," Ailey smiled.

Taps's face lost some of its sparkle. "He was just being nice. That's all. Everybody says he's a real nice man."

"Well, he's a real nice man who wants to see you. You'll do great, I know it." Ailey followed Taps across one lively street and down another. He took everything in, locking it all in his memory.

"Up this way," Tap said, climbing the steps of the Harlem subway station.

"The A train," Ailey laughed, remembering. "Hurry, hurry, hurry. Take the A train / To get to Sugar Hill way up in Harlem," he sang out, smiling. "Grampa used to *always* play this. Duke Ellington, I think."

"Don't think I've ever heard it. And I listen to everything he's got," Taps said.

"Maybe it hasn't come out yet, who knows. But when it does, you'll love it."

Taps dropped a nickel into the turnstile and was about to hand Ailey one.

"Uh, uh, uh." Ailey shook his head. "I got this." He pulled a nickel from his pocket. "You're not the only one who's gotten coins for his moves." He raised his eyebrows up and down, spinning in his footsies. Then he pushed through the turnstile and followed Taps up to the train platform.

"What's he like?" Taps asked, as they waited for the next train.

"Who?" Ailey shouted, as subway cars rattled by on the opposite track.

"Your grandpa." Taps pushed his cap back and scratched his forehead.

"He's amazing." Ailey's smile filled his face. "The smartest person I know, besides my mom. He knows everything. And can do anything." Ailey stretched his arms out wide.

"I mean without his tappin'?" asked Taps, stepping forward as the train doors opened.

"Oh." Ailey went still. Then rushed behind Taps onto the train. "I guess he's okay," Ailey said a second later. His gaze drifted up over all the old advertisements running the length of the train car. "Or at least that's what I thought before I knew about these . . ." Ailey lifted one of the shoes he'd draped around his neck by knotting the shoelaces together. "I would've thought he was super happy. But now I'm not so sure. Uncle Sammy says he misses tapping like a dried up pond misses water, and now I think he might be right." Ailey thought about how alive and free Taps looked when he tapped. Like it was the only thing worth doing in the world. "He keeps the shoes in a box of regret."

"A box of what?"

"Regret. He regrets not getting up on the stage." Ailey dragged his foot back and forth across the subway floor. The bottoms of his footsies, shredded.

"Regrets, regrets/Regret's nothin' nice . . ."

Taps whispered and shoved a hand in his pocket as the train jostled them back and forth. Ailey watched scenes of Harlem passing in each window.

"Hey, Taps," he said a few seconds later.

"Yeah?" Taps lifted his eyes, not his head.

"I want you to have this." Ailey pulled at the band of his Black Panther watch, unfastening it.

"What for?" Taps didn't take it.

"Luck," Ailey said. "And strength. It'll remind you that you have strength too. Maybe not as much as a superhero, but you have it. Let it remind you that you can be strong."

Taps stared at the watch in Ailey's hand. No one on the train paid them any mind. "You know I'm not gonna take that, right?"

"I knew you'd say that." Ailey grinned. "But technically

since you gave it to me, I'm just giving it back." Ailey's grin grew.

Taps narrowed his gaze, studying Ailey. "You really think I'm gonna ever believe you traveled back in time to help little ole me?"

"It doesn't actually matter anymore," Ailey said. "What's important is that you believe you can get up on that stage. *With one breath, and one step*—" He thrust the watch at Taps. "Just take it. You can give it back after your audition."

Ailey could tell Taps wanted it. He dangled it in front of him until the corner of Taps's mouth turned up.

"Deal." Taps secured the watch to his wrist, holding his arm up to admire it. "Snaps! This is us . . . let's go." They dashed off the train, almost missing their stop at 42nd Street.

CHAPTER THIRTY-FIVE

A PERSON COULD LOSE MORE THAN JUST BREAKFAST

As Ailey and Taps followed the stream of people out of the station, Taps stared down at the watch like it would disappear if he didn't keep his eye on it.

The sun shined brightly as they strolled along Eighth Avenue. Ailey mumbled their rap, then Taps joined in.

> *On this stage,*
> *Fear ain't got no room.*
> *See, this is my cue to tap my feet and do what I do.*
> *One breath, one step*
> *This is my chance to do my best.*

Taps's voice faded and he stopped suddenly, like he'd hit a glass wall. Ailey collided into him.

"What's wrong?" Ailey said, regaining his balance. His eyes roamed the area in search of Bumpy or some other trouble. "Wait." He pointed. "Is that it?" Across the street, a large brick building, curved at its corner, stared back at them. Ailey wasn't sure it was the right one until he looked over the doors. A single painted word shined in the glass. *Broadhurst.*

Taps didn't answer, he just stared ahead. Ailey stepped to the edge of the curb. They were really here. Grampa could change his stars.

"Maybe I should come back tomorrow or another day." Taps backed away from the edge of the sidewalk. "He probably isn't even here on a Sunday."

"Come on. It doesn't hurt to check." Ailey nudged Taps. "You told me he's always practicing. Always trying to get it right. He'll be there."

Taps suddenly looked like he couldn't hold his breakfast.

Ailey hesitated only a split second before pulling him across the street. This was his shot.

"So this is it?" Ailey said. Not wasting a second, he sauntered over and yanked a door, but it didn't budge. He tugged again.

"See," Taps said, sounding a bit relieved. "I told you it'd be closed today."

Ailey rattled the door again. "It can't be." He pulled harder. Then his hands dropped. He raced toward the other entrance.

"Leave it." Taps didn't chase him.

Ailey jerked the other doors. They rattled but didn't open.

"Hey, young man, they're not going to budge." A man with smoothed down waves leaned against the light pole near the entrance. Peanut shells littered the ground around him. "They're padlocked from the inside. You need to go around that way. To the backstage door." The man pointed toward the alley at the side of the building. "That's open."

It took less than half a second for Ailey to lock onto Taps's arm and run. "Thanks, Mister," he shouted behind them, dragging Taps along. "Come on. Let's go."

The alley was short and narrow. The two buildings and the fire escape over them blocked out most of the early afternoon light.

"Move it, slowpoke." Ailey tugged on Taps and didn't quit until they reached the backstage door. He stared up at the plain black door as if it were the entrance to another galaxy—or Oz. He suddenly knew how Dorothy, the Scarecrow, and the others must have felt when they thought their hopes were about to come true.

He hesitated, uncertain. Panic nipped his heels. And excitement exploded like popcorn kernels inside him. Taps hung back.

This was it.

Ailey closed his eyes for a second, then he grasped the

handle. Cold metal pressed against his sweaty palm. A rush of air hit them when he opened the door.

A giant, broader than the door and taller than a bulldozer, stepped forward. He was dressed in all black, a fedora tittering to the side of his string bean-like head. Ailey gaped.

"Ex-cu-se me, sir," he stuttered. "But my—friend needs to go inside."

"Who you here to see?" The deep voice rattled the landing and Ailey's bones.

"The Mayor of Harlem, The King of Tap, Mr. Bojangles," Ailey rambled.

The mammoth's mouth twitched. Almost like he wanted to smile. "I can't let you in."

"Come on, Ailey. Let's go," Taps suggested. "I told you it wasn't the right time to come."

"It is," Ailey argued. "It has to be!"

He turned away from Taps and stood face to belt buckle with the giant. Even on tiptoes, he would have only reached his enormous belly.

Taps sucked in a breath.

"Mister, he's supposed to be here." Ailey shoved Taps forward and lifted Bojangles's shoes. "Mr. Bojangles gave him his shoes. He told him to come."

"Munch." The man who'd pointed them to the backdoor came down the alley. "They're good. Let 'em in."

"It's on you, Maurice." The giant stepped aside enough for a crack of light to appear behind him. To Ailey it looked like what his Sunday School teacher described as the light to paradise.

"Follow me." But before they could even make it a step inside, the giant held up his hand. Ailey's forehead met a pasty palm. "Show some respect." His eyes burrowed into Ailey. "No one's getting in to see the Mayor without shoes on his feet!"

Ailey opened his mouth to explain but slammed it closed. He couldn't risk the giant changing his mind about letting them in. Without another thought, he undid the laces and scrambled into Bojangles's oversize shoes. At his side, Taps went from looking sick to looking like he was about to wet himself, fidgeting back and forth.

Once Ailey had tied the laces as tightly as he could, even then it was useless, he squeezed Taps's arm to get him to move again. "You got this," Ailey whispered.

A thin vein pulsed at the side of Tap's neck.

It was now or never.

Ailey held his breath and took the first step.

This time, Taps stuck to him like *he* was gum and Ailey was the shoe.

CHAPTER THIRTY-SIX

THE BEGINNING OF
THE REST OF YOUR LIFE

Ailey and Taps pressed close together, trudging forward. They followed the lumbering giant down a dark, smoke-filled hallway. The walls pushed in on them as they went deeper into the theater. Munch's sides grazed the wallpaper. Ailey was sure he would get stuck or, worse, squish someone as they made their way down the corridor. Taps rubbed his thumb across the face of Ailey's watch like Ailey sometimes did when he was nervous. Ailey craned his neck to see inside each open doorway. In one, a woman fixed her lipstick, winking as they passed. And in another, a man leaned back in a chair, feet crossed on the dressing table, reading a magazine.

Ailey's heart did a fast but rhythmic beat in his ears. As they neared the back of the stage, the floor bounced to the melody of a song being banged out on a nearby piano.

"Let's take it from the top," someone shouted as Ailey

and Taps were ushered past a red velvet curtain to the side of the stage. The music stopped as soon as they stepped out from behind the camouflage of dark.

A group of performers stood at center stage. They hung on each other. Their chests rose and fell together. They looked as if they'd collapse at any moment, but as soon as the music started again, they pranced around like sugar-fueled puppets on strings.

"What do we have here?" A man strolled down the center aisle. His white teeth sparkled against his dark brown skin. Ailey recognized him instantly. It was Bojangles.

"I had nothing to do with it, boss," Munch said, holding up his hands. He backed away and disappeared.

Out of the corner of his eye, Ailey saw Taps twisting the watchband on his wrist like Ailey *always* did when he was nervous.

"Um . . . Mr. Bojangles, sir." Ailey stepped forward. A few people snickered and pointed at his feet. Then there was a hushed whisper in the theater when Mr. Robinson looked around. "Sorry to disturb you, sir." Ailey had never spoken with a real star before. Not a human one, anyway. His stomach plummeted to his knees and a lump the size of a meteor lodged in his throat. "You told my, um, friend to come see you when he was ready to bring back the tap shoes you gave him." Ailey glanced at his own feet, then gave Taps a gentle push forward. "And for him to show you what he's got."

Bojangles stood right below the stage, his large eyes taking them in. "Is that true, son? Did I say, come show me what you got? Is he telling it right?"

Taps bit at the inside of his cheek.

"Speak up, son." Bojangles spun his hands up, as if asking for the volume to be raised. "Everything's *copasetic* 'round here."

"Come on," Ailey whispered. "This is your chance."

"*Bwok-bwok-bwok,*" hit Ailey's ears. It was faint and quick, but he heard it. His eyes zipped to the back of the theater and spotted King, Zee, and a few older people lounging in a row off to the side. And Franny. Franny was there, too, sitting right next to King.

Ailey's breath caught. *This can't be happening. Not today.*

"This isn't a farm. There aren't any chickens in here." The Mayor snapped his fingers over his head, never turning from Taps. There was instant silence. "You there, son . . ." His smile was bright and warm. "You ready to show me what you got?"

"No regrets, remember?" Ailey said. "*This is your chance to do what you do.*"

It was almost as if Taps were stone. He didn't even blink.

"As I recall, you wouldn't accept my gift. You bringing my taps back to me?" Bojangles joked, then peeked over at Ailey's feet. Taps said nothing. "I'll be kind of offended if you don't answer me, son." His voiced turned a little stern, but Ailey could tell he didn't really mean it.

"Yes, sir." Taps mumbled, politeness besting nerves. "They've never left my side." His eyes darted to Ailey.

"I was just keeping them warm for you, sir." Ailey smiled and bent to take them off even though he didn't want to.

"We'll come to that later," Bojangles said, motioning for Ailey to stand back up. "Right now, I'm hoping he came to tap. Didn't you, son?"

Taps nodded slightly and pulled at the strap of his burlap sack. He took out his own tap shoes and let the sack drop to the floor. He unlaced his shoes and then slid into his taps. Everyone in the theater waited. There wasn't a sound except for Taps's rustling. It took an eternity for him to lace up his shoes because his hands shook so much.

"Ready?" Bojangles asked, when he'd finally finished and stood.

In a matter of seconds, Taps had become a statue again. Bojangles moved forward, talking low so only Taps could hear.

"*Bwok-bwok*," rang out again, like a quick jab.

Ailey blinked, glaring at the back of the theater. He hustled off the stage and slosh-charged up the side aisle toward King and his friends, trying not to trip out of the shoes. There was no way he was going to let King ruin Taps's big moment.

"What are you doing here?" Ailey barked at King, not looking at Franny.

"Please," King smirked. "I'm here all the time. I know people." He nodded down the row. A few people wore leotards, but they all had on dance shoes. Except King, Zee, and Franny. "I got an open invite from my cuz here to come whenever I want. The question is what are *you* doing here?" His arm rested comfortably on the back of Franny's chair.

"You know what we're doing," Ailey said. He stood as tall as he could. He felt Franny's eyes on him and looked her way. "Taps got invited by the Mayor himself. The day he wasn't interested in you or your tapping, remember?" He swerved his head toward King.

King sucked his teeth. "Whatever, Ducky."

Franny searched Ailey's face like she hadn't heard him right, then she looked past him to Taps.

King snickered. "But that don't tell me why he's here though. I keep telling you, he always chokes when folks is watchin'."

"No, he doesn't," Ailey shot back. "He taps for crowds all the time."

"That's 'cause no one important is lookin'." King lifted a finger. "You'll see."

"Yeah," Zee chimed in. "You'll see." He wrapped his hands around his throat like he was gagging, stuck out his tongue, and rolled his eyes toward the sky.

King and everyone around him tittered. Everyone except Franny. Her eyes stayed on Taps as if she were trying to push him into motion with her thoughts.

"Not this time." Ailey hoped he sounded certain, but glancing back at a stone Taps, a small part of him worried. *Taps didn't look so good.*

"Quiet back there," the Mayor demanded. "I ain't havin' no noise. And if you aren't in one of the next acts, you might be needin' to go." He stared directly at King, who slipped a little deeper in his chair. "Work's 'bout to be done up here. Isn't it, son?" He turned back to Taps.

Ailey crashed into a seat a few rows ahead of King and Franny. He watched Taps, who still hadn't moved.

"Take your time. Feel that rhythm and that beat." Bojangles snapped his fingers again and did a *pa-tap*, *tap*, *tap*. His legs hardly moved as he tapped. But the sound traveled the theater as if five people danced. "Turn off that radio."

There were too many people. Ailey knew Taps couldn't focus. Knew he couldn't turn off the noise.

"Told you he was going to choke," King said, louder than any whisper Ailey had ever heard. But not loud enough to reach Mr. Robinson's ears.

"Stop it," Franny snapped. "At least he's up on the stage trying, and not just sitting around flapping his trap, bull-skating."

Ailey grinned when Franny removed King's arm from the top of her chair. He thought of something Grampa always said about her. *She could have told me to dive into the ocean and bring back the sun on the horizon, and I would have tried. I would have done anything she wanted me to.*

"Franny," Ailey whispered, calling her forward in her seat. "You have to help him. He'll listen to anything you tell him. He loves you. He has since the day you moved to his building. He says your smile could give breath for a thousand years or something."

"*Yuck!*" King gagged.

Franny elbowed him, cutting her eyes his way, then bent closer to Ailey. "Did he really say that?" She looked up at the stage toward a frozen Taps.

Ailey nodded. "Come and help me get him to try." She grabbed Ailey's hand, and they both sprang to their feet and raced down the aisle and up the steps at the side of the stage. There was no time for hesitation.

CHAPTER THIRTY-SEVEN

IT TOOK MORE
THAN JUST DOROTHY ON THAT
YELLOW BRICK ROAD

Ailey marched onto the stage, Franny beside him. He stood squarely in front of Taps. Close enough that he and Franny hopefully blocked Taps's view of Bojangles and everyone else.

"No regrets, remember?" Ailey said. "Come on, Grampa." He prodded Taps. "We didn't come this far to fail."

Taps didn't meet his gaze. But when Franny stepped closer, his eyes immediately found hers. His whole face lifted like it had in the hospital and on the fire escape, but he didn't smile. She reached on her tiptoes and kissed his cheek. When she moved away, his eyes still tracked her. She whispered, "Tap for me. I wanna see you dance, *Benjiman*."

Taps blinked, pressing his hand to where she'd kissed him. His eyes were still on her as she took a half step back. For a nanosecond he wasn't a statue.

Ailey pounced.

"*Regrets, regrets/Regret's nothin' nice . . .*" He shook Taps's arm, improvising a little. "*Check one, check two/See, this is your cue/Tap your feet and do what I do.*" Ailey tapped like Taps had shown him. He was a little wobbly in the shoes, but he had to try. *Rappitty-tap-tap, rappitty-tap-tap.*

Taps's eyes lowered, trained on Ailey's feet. Then he looked directly in Ailey's eyes. His own pleaded for him to stop.

Ailey ignored them. "*Right now, it's all on you to be all you can be,*" Ailey whispered. His feet slapped the stage.

"Whatcha doin' there, son?" Bojangles asked behind him.

Ailey hated to ignore him, but he did. He didn't want to break eye contact with Taps, who blinked when Ailey blinked. Ailey tapped lightly, as if testing a frozen lake. He made sure he remained between Taps and where Bojangles stood. Making sure King and Zee couldn't be seen either. His feet went *kertap-tap-tap* and *ba-dap-dap-dap*. Then he ran in place, his taps knocking against the wood planks of the stage.

Taps's eyelids fluttered fast, as if sweeping dust from his eyes.

"*With one breath and one step/This is your chance to do your best,*" Ailey urged. He swung his feet in small, slight circles, but he kept his eyes on Taps while Taps's eyes remained glued to Ailey's. Taps had shown Ailey how to sweep his leg across the ground like a paintbrush, so Ailey tried it. Taps had taught Ailey a simple ball change move, so Ailey tried that too. *Bu-dump-shh, bu-dump-shh.* His left heel kept grazing the stage. But it didn't matter. It was coaxing Taps out of his fog.

"What are you doing?" Taps tried to look around Ailey, but Ailey mirrored his movements, blocking his view.

"*With Sammy's grit . . .*" Ailey continued, hoping Taps would tap out the correct moves like he'd done all day. As if bashful, Taps's eyes slide to Franny for a quick second. "Show him how it's done," she whispered.

"*And shinin' stars,*" Ailey prompted when Taps looked back. Taps did the simple ball change Ailey couldn't seem to do.

"*It'll be easier in the end . . .*"

Ka-tap-tap-tap. Bu-dap-dap-dap. Taps's feet patted the stage. "*And not as hard,*" he mumbled and kept going when Ailey started the rhyme over. "*Regrets, regrets/Regret's nothin' nice.*"

Rap-a-tap-tap. Rap-a-tap-tap. Taps glided in an easy shuffle, back and forth like a rocked baby.

"You got this, Grampa," Ailey whispered when Taps spoke louder. With more grit.

"On this stage fear ain't got no room."

Taps continued shuffling, finding his beat. Then he hopped over one leg and then the other. He did a *bitty-bitty-bop* and a *kerpac-kerpac-kerpac*, lost in the rhythm and the song. Ailey and Franny sidestepped to the corner of the stage and watched Taps dance, face glowing. Ailey knew Taps no longer saw anyone. That he'd gotten lost in the beat. That he'd turned off the radio. Everyone leaned forward, all eyes locked on Taps's feet. *Clickitty-clac, clickitty-clac, clickitty-clickitty-clickitty-clac-clac-clac.*

"Yes!" Ailey whispered.

Bojangles chuckled. "Alright, alright! You're doin' it now, son." He clapped his hands, then swung his arm, catching Taps's beat. Once he caught it, he tapped along. *Bipitty-bap, bibitty-bap.* Mimicking Taps's steps.

Every part of Taps joined in the dance. His movements were slight, but connected. Even his eyebrows shifted with the beat.

Nothing held him back.

Ailey glanced down at Bojangles's shoes, shining like they'd just been polished. Looking back at Taps, he smiled and whispered. "That's it, Grampa. No regrets."

CHAPTER THIRTY-EIGHT

THERE'S NO PLACE LIKE HOME

There was no rumble, no crackle, and certainly no pop. Only a tightening of laces and a slurping of leather around his feet.

The shoes *were* magic.

When Ailey opened his eyes, everything was a haze. The space around him rippled and fluttered like a wave. Silence met his ears. His legs buckled and he almost crashed to the ground.

An unfamiliar ground.

"Hello?" His voice rang out in the hollow space.

No reply.

He blinked a hundred times. Only blotches of color and light flashed around him.

The whoosh of what sounded like a ceiling fan was all he heard. A cool breeze sweeping across his head. He rubbed at his eyes, hoping to see the shelves of the hardware store's office, the Broadhurst stage, or something familiar.

Anything. But when the walls came into focus, nothing was the same.

Where was he?

He spun, searching for familiar.

Nothing.

Not one single thing.

A wall-to-ceiling mirror stretched the length of the room. A piano rested in the corner. He couldn't tell if it was old or new.

He stood in the middle of a polished parquet floor. *Had the shoes taken him to the wrong place?*

Panic zipped through him like pinballs.

He scanned the room. *There has to be something I know.* But there was hardly anything in the space. A small couch and plant hunched in an alcove at the side. Tall speakers stood watch in two corners.

Where was he?

He just wanted home.

The shoes were still snug around his feet and the laces tightly knotted. But something had gone wrong. Terribly wrong.

The pesky worms in his gut told him he'd never see Grampa, Taps, or any of his family ever again. Ailey wobbled.

His eyes kept searching. Refusing to give up. Then they locked on the wall above the couch. Black frames crammed the bricks between two windows showing a late morning sky. Ailey twisted. Photographs and articles in simple frames in every shape and size crowded the brick. But a large, fancy gold frame stood in the center of it all. He ran forward, hopeful.

In a brownish photograph that stared out at Ailey, the Taps Ailey knew danced alongside the Mayor of Harlem, circled by a crowd of cheering onlookers. "To Taps, Thanks for turning off the noise so we could make the music, Wonder Boy. With best wishes always, Uncle Bo" was scrawled in black ink across the corner in cursive. When Ailey leaned in closer, air caught in his throat.

Naw? Squinting, he saw himself in the crowd. Dressed exactly as he was right then.

"How?" Ailey whispered to the image, then remembered Zee snapping pictures every time he saw him.

Ailey studied the wall. Black and white and old colored photos, framed *Playbills*, newspaper clippings, and magazine spreads welcomed his gaze. Taps smiled from different stages and wore flashy costumes. Other grinning faces surrounded him. Articles about "Taps, The Wonder Boy" drew Ailey's attention. Then it took him a second to register a picture he saw. An image of Taps and King tapping together, all smiles.

"Sweet!" Ailey pumped his fist in the air. It had worked. He'd done it. Grampa had done it. He had changed his stars.

Ailey stared in awe, reading the captions underneath.

Taps had traveled to Tokyo, Havana, Los Angeles, Boston, Detroit, and many other places in between. He'd seen the world because of his tapping.

A picture Ailey had seen before, hanging on the wall by Grampa's workbench, had changed slightly. Gone was the red and white striped awning over the building's front doors. A black awning with the words *Skygazer Dance Studio*, written in white cursive letters had replaced *Lane Family Hardware*. An outline of a dancer in a top hat and a tuxedo with tails that swirled around him was painted in white on the window. Sparkling stars haloed him. Grampa and Gramma Franny still hugged, smiling near the doors like in the image Ailey remembered, but Grampa's old orange pickup had also been replaced with his favorite powder blue '53 Chevy.

Ailey grinned, remembering Gramma Franny coming to sit on the fire escape and Taps's goofy smile when she kissed him at the theater. Ailey reached in his pocket and felt the fabric flower she'd given him.

He let out a long, deep sigh. One he'd held since he first went back in time.

He thought he'd never get back home. *But was he?*

"There you are, Jackrabbit . . . well, I'll be." Grampa slowed in the doorway. Not twelve-year-old Taps, but Grampa—cane-holding, gray-haired Grampa, although the cane was gone. "I knew this was supposed to happen one day. But I gotta say I didn't all the way believe it 'til right now . . ." His voice trailed off as he studied every inch of Ailey. "If my own eyes weren't tellin' me so, I'm not sure I'd trust this. You standing here."

"Grampa . . ." Ailey rushed into his arms before Grampa could steady himself. They almost tumbled over. "Is it really you?" Ailey buried his face in the scratchy wool of Grampa's sweater that smelled of Old Spice and spearmints. It was him. And he wasn't in the hospital anymore. He was right there with Ailey.

"Is it really you? That's the question." Grampa shook his head as he patted Ailey on the cheek and chuckled. Like he was checking to see if he was real.

Ailey pressed his head deeper into Grampa's chest.

"We better head on up, 'fore your mom turns over Josephine's cake or calls somebody, looking for you." Grampa started leading Ailey toward the side door. "Don't ask me why, but I had an inklin' this was about the time you were due for a little unexpected travel, so I told her you skipped over real early to play video games with that friend of yours, Maceo. I don't like fibbin', but this time it was necessary." He winked.

Maceo, Ailey thought. *He'd never believe this.* Then Ailey smiled, knowing this was a secret he and Grampa would keep to themselves forever.

"The party's just starting, so you better rush up and change out of these things. You know, I didn't tell you back then, but you can see the imprint of the Black Panther union suit under that getup of yours."

Ailey looked down and then at the wall-length mirror and, sure enough, through the thin cotton fabric of his shirt he could see the Black Panther's mighty chest. He should've felt embarrassed, but his smile grew even wider. Then he thought about everything Grampa had said.

"Wait? Jojo's party?" he said, more to himself than Grampa, realizing, *It hadn't been canceled, because Grampa was okay.*

Ailey hugged Grampa tighter, never wanting to let go.

"Of course," Grampa said, hugging back. "You know nothing would stop your sister from celebrating the day *she blessed us all*, as she puts it." His chest vibrated against Ailey's ear from laughter. "Gotta love that chil'. Now go on up, get changed. Truth be told, I think Jojo wants you there. She done asked about you more than once this morning."

"*My* sister?" Ailey said, not believing.

"*Your* sister. She sure looked just as nervous as your mom when they realized you weren't asleep on the air mattress under Uncle Sammy's crusty feet." Bojangles's shoes clinked against the floorboards as they crossed the room. Grampa's gaze dropped to them. "I can't believe it. Haven't seen those in a long, long time." And as if the shoes understood they'd

265

helped fulfill a wish, the laces slipped out of their tight knots, and rested against the floor.

Grampa and Ailey both stared.

Ailey waited for the shoes to spring back to their original size, and Grampa was simply lost in amazement.

"Well, I never," Grampa said as Ailey pulled his foot out of the still form-fitting shoes.

Ailey bent down and picked them up. "I think I'm supposed to give these back to you."

"No, Jackrabbit." Grampa shook his head. "Those look meant for you. Besides, my stars are right where they need to be."

A bit relieved, Ailey held the shoes close, not sure why, but not quite ready to part with them.

"Come on now, no time for dillydallying. Your mom might come charging any second or, worse, call Maceo's mom." Grampa popped a spearmint in his mouth, offering another to Ailey. "Right now, it's time to cut a little rug." Grampa did a little tap. "And party!"

Ailey's whole chest warmed.

Grampa tapped.

CHAPTER THIRTY-NINE

IT'S A FAMILY AFFAIR

Music hopped down the stairs before Ailey and Grampa even reached the apartment door. Ailey was sure Dad was set up with his turntables and laptop like every year, giving everyone a show like he said he had in college. Secretly Ailey had always thought his dad liked these birthday parties more than he and Jojo did.

When Grampa pushed open the door, tangerine fabric draped the ceiling and rippled down the walls like a fancy desert tent. Golden stars huge from clear string, and Moroccan lamps glowed like mini fires hanging on metal links around the room and on fabric-covered tables. *Streamers and balloons were never enough for Jojo. She always had to be so EXTRA.* Ailey's dad tipped his head to him from behind the makeshift DJ booth, speakers pulsing at his sides. Ailey was glad to hear he still had skills.

"Where in heaven's name have you been, young man?"

His mom's hands settled on her hips. She was a wall in front of him. "I was about to call Maceo's mother if you didn't get back here soon."

So much for sneaking upstairs unnoticed.

"Boy, what do you have on? And what in the world happened to your feet?

Before Ailey remembered who he was talking to, he said, "It's a long story." He could feel his tattered footsies peeking out from under his pants legs.

"Well, you know I have time to hear it once you change for your sister's party."

Ailey glanced over at Grampa, who winked as Ailey headed for the stairs. "Not sure it's that interesting." He couldn't help but smile.

"If you say so." Her A.L.D. working overtime. "Oh, and another thing," she said, pointing toward Ailey as he took the steps two at a time. "If you ever think about leaving this house again at the crack of dawn without kissing me good morning first and letting your dad and me see your brilliant face—*don't!*" She arched an eyebrow. "You get me?"

"Yes, ma'am," Ailey droned. This was home.

As soon as he pushed open the door to his bedroom, lazy King, who never moved faster than a snail unless a treat was involved, rocketed off Ailey's bed. That too was a surprise, because he never got on Ailey's bed—it required too much energy.

But before Ailey could fully step into his room, King swooshed around his legs, looking overjoyed to see him. Ailey bent down, placing Bojangles's tap shoes on the floor, as King licked his face. "I actually missed you too," Ailey said, smashing his head against King's neck.

Although Ailey's room looked basically the same, like King, certain things were slightly different. Taps, in costume, stared out from a large poster on the wall, and on his desk a picture frame held an image of a smiling Taps, Bojangles, King, Franny, and a group of others. A couple pair of well-loved tap shoes, one pair in gold, were lined in the corner.

Ailey flopped back on his bed, taking it all in. King jumped up beside him. "I really did it, boy. I really helped Grampa change his stars."

After lying there for a few minutes looking up at the stars across his ceiling, Ailey pulled himself up. All he wanted was to sleep, but he also wanted to be with family. He emptied his pockets, finding Franny's flower, the crumpled pages of the Crow's Anthem, and his iPod. The first thing he did was plug in his Nano to make sure it still worked, then he opened up the mashed-up paper. He wished he could have a

second chance at the Scarecrow, but knew that wasn't going to happen, so he would just make sure he'd be ready for the next opportunity that came his way. He would practice!

He grabbed his towel and darted to the bathroom. After a night in a doorway, he could definitely use a shower. Besides, his smell would not get past his mom, and she would have a million more questions.

Fresh and changed, he headed back downstairs, King close at his side. Jojo was in the middle of the room, a bright lantern over her head like a spotlight. *Of course.*

She danced with friends to a mash-up recording of her playing Vivaldi's *La Serenissima* on her violin with hip-hop beats Dad added booming from the speakers.

"There you go," Mom said, opening her arm so Ailey could tuck himself against her. "I'm glad you made it and that I didn't have to come get you." She swayed to the beat, kissing the top of his head.

"He's home now, Billie. Let the boy be. Why don't you go over there and show the girls how it's done?" He nodded toward the makeshift dance floor.

"*Huumphh,* you're right, Daddy," she sighed, pecking his cheek and giving Ailey a last squeeze. Then she snapped her fingers and sashayed onto the dance floor. Jojo and her friends squealed and hollered, surrounding her, as they all swung their hips in unison.

When Jojo saw Ailey, she lifted an eyebrow and twisted her mouth up like she was fighting off a grin. Ailey knew it was the closest thing to a smile he'd get from her. And he'd take it.

As the song wound down she came over to him, passing Uncle Sammy snoring in a recliner with King curled by his feet.

"Where've you been?" She crossed her arms over her bedazzled sweatshirt that read: *Lay all presents before the feet of the Queen!*

"Around," Ailey said again.

"What *around* here is more important than my party?" Her neck and chin jutted forward.

"I thought you wanted a "grown-up" party. Without me bothering you."

"Like you ever listen to me."

It took all his willpower not to reach out and hug her. Then he remembered. "I have something for you," he said as she fluffed up her poufy turquoise tutu. He pulled Franny's flower out of his pocket. "Happy Birthday. Sorry it's not wrapped."

She stared at it, bringing it close to her face. "Where'd you get this?" She slid her thumb across the delicate fabric.

"From a friend. Thought you might like it."

Jojo twirled the flower in her hand. The petals fluttered as if winking. "Thanks," she said, looking just as surprised as Ailey, because she actually sounded like she meant it. She held the turquoise flower up against the turquoise of her skirt.

"Look at that," Grampa said, squinting. "It's like it was made for you." He leaned closer. "Haven't seen a flower like that in years."

"At least it's one thing he didn't screw up," Jojo said over her shoulder as she paraded back to her friends. She pushed the flower into the tiara she wore. Then she glanced back at Ailey, sticking out her tongue.

Things had changed, but he was definitely home.

CHAPTER FORTY

SOMETIMES THE TOUGHEST CRITIC IS THE STRONGEST SUPPORT

"Okay, we're ready." Ailey's mom slapped her hands together as she sat on the couch next to his dad. Jojo was tucked on the floor next to King, her violin resting on top of its turquoise case. "Show us what you're workin' wit," mom said.

"Come on now." Grampa and Uncle Sammy slapped their knees at the same time.

Ailey stared at all of them staring at him. He still reeled from the fact that he'd actually made it through to callbacks. Or at least the Ailey *who was born tapping* hadn't botched things up. He'd done what *time-traveling Ailey* couldn't, and he'd even sung. And supposedly he was tough competition for Mahalia. Ailey had secretly hoped great singing hadn't followed her into this present. *But no one was that lucky.* So he didn't have to ask for a second chance. He just needed to find a way not to mess this one up.

"What are you waiting for?" Jojo sighed. She tapped her bow once against her forehead. "I want to play the new song I made."

"You're up next," Dad said, tickling her foot with his sock-covered toes.

She giggled.

Ailey took a deep breath. He could do this.

Grampa's eyes crinkled at the corners. He was the only one who understood this was the *old* Ailey. The one who froze when people watched. The one who wasn't born tapping. But this Grampa also knew he could do it. The rug was still rolled in the corner from Jojo's party the night before. And Ailey had slipped back into Bojangles's shoes. They fit like they waited for him. The taps clinked against the hard wood. When he closed his eyes, he tried to block everything, but doubt and uncertain thoughts played louder in his head. Then Jojo jumped up.

"Let's do it together," she suggested, grabbing her violin.

"You know the Crow's Anthem?" he asked.

"*Of course.*" She rested the violin on her neck and collarbone ready to play. "You've blasted it a gazillion times!"

When she started, Ailey closed his eyes again, this time concentrating on the vibration through the floor, not his doubt. His feet did a *clickitty-clickitty-clac* and a *rap-a-tap-tap*. After a deep breath, he was ready to try his rhyme.

"Wake up, sweetheart. You don't want to be late." Ailey's mom shook his bed and ruffled his sheets Monday morning.

"Late?" Ailey popped up. "What time is it?" He scratched his neck under the collar of his freshly washed Black Panther PJs. A good luck charm his mom wanted to toss when he'd asked her to wash them the night before. He spilled out of bed tangled in the sheets, Bojangles's tap shoes—another of his good luck charms—still on his feet.

"Take it easy." His mom steadied him as he almost toppled over trying to hide the shoes from her. "You aren't late yet, but this is the third time I've called you." She gathered up the sheets from around his legs. "Boy, why are you wearing shoes?"

"I must've fallen asleep in them." Ailey could see her A.L.D. working.

His mom studied him then the shoes. "Where'd they come from? Never seen them before."

"Just some old taps of Grampa's." He looked down. "I feel like they bring me luck."

"You've been practicing forever. You don't need luck." She watched him. "You nervous?"

"A little." Ailey refused to admit just how much. Everyone

already thought he could do it. And that almost felt worse. No one expected him to fail.

"You've got this." She licked her finger, rubbing at the crust at the corner of his eye. Normally he would worm away, but today he loved it, saliva and all.

"I guess," Ailey said a bit unsure. He thought about Grampa telling him late into the night to take it slow. Grampa had pointed to Ailey's head and the tip of his shoe then said, "You got it all right here and here."

But that didn't stop his nerves from taking over. He wanted this all to go so right. He needed to make his audition great. And if the Mahalia in his new life was anything like the Mahalia in his old one, he needed to be better than great.

His mom lifted his face so their eyes met. "You'll do wonderful. Now go get ready and come down for breakfast. You have a big day ahead." When she got to the doorway she slowed. "I'm proud of you," she smiled. "No matter what."

He hoped she'd still say that after 4 p.m.

CHAPTER FORTY-ONE

LEAVING IT ALL ON THE STAGE

At school the audition was the only thing anyone talked about all day. Teachers kept shushing students and telling them to get back to work in—Every. Single. Class.

At lunch all anyone talked about was *The Wiz*.

Even though costumes weren't required for callbacks, almost everyone wore one. Even a simple one, like an all-silver tracksuit, a gray skully, and gray, fingerless weightlifter's gloves like Dewey wore. Ailey thought he better not chance it though and kept his costume tucked away in his locker.

He wanted to save the wow for when he got on the stage. His costume was EVERYTHING! After all, his mom was a seamstress and costume designer, just like Gramma Franny, her mother, Mrs. Criss, Great-great Nanna Truth, and Great-gramma Zelda. There was no way she wasn't going to make him a *baaad* costume. He thought of his Harlem family and smiled.

When he'd pulled on his outfit in a bathroom stall and finally made it to the auditorium—his jitters were just warming up. Everyone sat around waiting. All tryouts were on the main stage. Hushed whispers and gasps echoed around Ailey as he made his way down the center aisle.

"Look at his costume. It's a perfect Scarecrow," someone said.

"Where'd his mom buy that?" another classmate wondered.

This time he didn't need fancy tricks like a dapper suit, he *was* the Scarecrow.

The Scarecrow tingled in every inch of his bones. His curls, picked high, Gramma Franny's old gardening hat slouched on his head. The patchwork overalls his mom had sewn swung loose, stuffed with newspaper and itchy hay sticking out from every direction. Jojo's face paint created his round black nose, and one of Grampa's stage jackets, freshly pressed and no longer smelling of mothballs, completed the look. It was definitely a family affair. But it wasn't the nose, the band jacket, or the overalls that drew the attention. It was Bojangles's shoes, shimmering and shining and clinking as he stepped.

Clic-clac, clic-clac, clic-clac.

"Well, Mr. Lane," Ms. Hansberry came up beside him. "Check you out."

Ailey beamed.

"Since you're the last to sign in, you'll be our final audition." She scribbled his name on her clipboard.

"Can you play this when it's my turn?" He held out a CD his dad and Jojo had put together, mixing hip-hop beats with Jojo's version of the Crow's Anthem.

Ms. Hansberry took the CD, directing him toward one of the rows. Then she headed for the stage. Her shoes were electric blue.

Someone in a lion costume a few rows farther up waved a paw at Ailey. It was Maceo with black painted-on whiskers and a pink nose. A burnt orange tutu that was probably his little sister's ringed his face. Ailey rushed to sit by his friend.

"Cool outfit," Maceo said when Ailey sat down.

"Yours too."

"So, did you figure out a way to make Jojo's cake explode when she blew out her candles?" Maceo whispered then glanced at Ailey's feet. "You're tapping?"

"Yeah, something a little different I wanted to add." He was bursting to tell his friend so much, but knew he never would.

"Quiet, you two." Ms. Hansberry put her finger up, then glanced at her clipboard. "First up is Ms. Jackson."

"*Agh*," Maceo grumbled. "All day she's been talking about *how she's going to be the Scarecrow*," he said in a mocking whine.

Ailey grinned, though his insides twisted a bit more. The pesky worms were back.

Ms. Hansberry settled behind the piano. "Do you have music for me today?"

"No," Mahalia said, then headed for the stage. "I'm going to perform a cappella. My mom and the children's choir director at my church said the power of my voice is stronger that way. It allows me to showcase my range."

"No, it allows her to showcase her big mouth," Ailey whispered to Maceo.

Maceo laughed behind a paw.

"Very well." Ms. Hansberry sat back on her piano stool. "Whenever you're ready then."

Mahalia cleared her throat.

Ailey's stomach burbled. Even though he couldn't stand her, he knew she *was* going to be good.

Mahalia's friends Kenya and Marisol rushed to the center of the stage. They weren't dressed as scarecrows like in the first audition. Instead they were pitch-black crows in black leotards with long orange poster-board beaks and capes strapped to their arms and shoulders to look like wings. A few long black feathers perched on their shoulders. Mahalia dragged over what looked like a tall cross attached to a box and stood on top of it. She had the same costume she'd worn before, but somehow it looked straight out of the movie. Not a costume shop. It seemed to have a Hollywood sparkle. Thanks to gold glitter she'd sprinkled all over herself, she twinkled under the lights as she moved.

Sneaky.

Ailey slumped back in his chair, remembering how Taps had shared Uncle Sammy's favorite saying: *You're your toughest competition.* He wished that were true.

As Mahalia belted out the song, Ailey bowed his head, looking away from the stage. Closing his eyes, he pressed his elbows against the armrest and burrowed his thumbs in his ears.

Let everything go, he heard Grampa say in his head. He lifted his feet and tapped, mumbling his rap.

Oh, can I win? Oh, can I win?

Instead of listening to Mahalia, he concentrated on the routine he'd practiced.

The routine he'd learned from Taps.

It wasn't perfect, but he was ready to try.

CHAPTER FORTY-TWO
TURN OFF THAT RADIO

"**H**ey, you're up." Maceo knocked Ailey's arm, sending it flying off the armrest.

"Uh? What?" Ailey opened his eyes, took his fingers out of his other ear and sat bolt straight. The students around him giggled.

"Wake up," Maceo whispered. An orange and brown Baltimore Black Sox baseball hat sat backward on his head under the tutu. Construction paper lion ears were stapled to the top. "It's your turn."

Ailey hadn't been asleep. He'd been playing his lines over and over in his head.

"Mr. Lane?" Ms. Hansberry watched him from the piano off to the side of the stage. "You ready?"

"I think so." Ailey pulled himself out of the chair. *You can do this*, he tried to convince himself but panic shadowed him, creeping along behind him up the steps.

Ms. Hansberry motioned toward the large *X* at the center

of the stage. "Whenever you're ready." Her hand hovered over the Play button for his CD.

When Ailey got to the mark, he looked around. Everyone stared his way. Some sat expressionless, while others smiled or stared, curious. The thought of Grampa on stage with King and Zee heckling him from the audience came to mind. He tried to block everything out and remember his lines.

Leave it on the stage.

His mind was crammed with all that had happened over the last two days. Days that had felt like a lifetime. The longer he stood motionless, the more the other students grew restless, and the whispers and giggles started.

Focus, Ailey. Focus. Ignore them.

But no matter what he told himself, his panic rose.

"I'll just start the music," Ms. Hansberry offered when he didn't give her a cue.

Classmates covered their mouths, but Ailey still heard their snickers.

Not again, he thought. His body wouldn't move. *You know this.*

"*Psst*," someone hissed from the side of the stage. "*Psst. Psst.*"

Ailey didn't budge.

"Come here, Jackrabbit." Ailey's head whisked to the side. Grampa stood deep in the curtains at the corner of the stage, out of sight.

Ailey glanced back out at everyone, then dashed over into Grampa's arms. The auditorium erupted in laughter. Ms. Hansberry demanded silence.

"That's enough," she said. "It's not easy getting up here. Give him a moment."

"What are you doing here? You're not supposed to be here, Grampa." Ailey whispered, but even as the words came out, he felt relieved to see him.

"*Psssh*. You think I was gonna miss your big audition? Never. Let someone tell me I gotta go. We made a deal, remember? I'm gonna see it through."

"I don't think I can do it," Ailey admitted.

Grampa lifted Ailey's chin. "Nonsense. You remember me on stage? Nearly scared the black off me."

Ailey actually felt a little stronger just remembering.

"Now when you get back out there, know you were born in this world tappin'. You had rhythm in the past, but you sure have some rhythm in your toes now."

Ailey looked down at his feet, calming himself. "I got this," he whispered.

"Yes, you do." Grampa nodded. "So, when you get out there simply close your eyes and wipe away the sound. *Turn off that radio*, like Uncle Bo taught us. Ain't nobody out there but you and that stage. Feel it in here." Grampa reached up and thumped his palm over Ailey's heart.

He stood up, hugged Ailey again, and fished for

something in his pocket. "Thought you might like to have this back." The Black Panther's muscled arms ticked around the watch face.

Ailey's mouth opened wide. "You kept it!"

"Of course, but remember, this doesn't hold the strength. You do." Ailey stared at the watch, then back up at Grampa who secured it around Ailey's wrist. "Now go out there and show 'em what you got. *Regrets, regrets. Regret's nothin' nice*." Grampa kissed Ailey's head and nudged him back on stage.

"*Check one, check two/On this stage, fear ain't got no room*," Ailey reminded himself.

Students stifled giggles and hushed each other as he headed back to the *X*.

Ms. Hansberry nodded toward Grampa, unnoticed by the students. She threw a stern look everyone's way, then smiled at Ailey. "You all set now?"

Ailey glanced back at Grampa, then nodded. He looked past the audience to the very last row.

He breathed in, closed his eyes, and rubbed his thumb across the watch's face. The low hum of Jojo's violin came over the speakers threaded with the deep bass of the hip-hop beat Dad had created. The rustle of his classmates' movements, the murmur of conversation, and the squeaking of unoiled hinges on seats came in and out, like someone played with the volume.

Tap-tap, tap-tap rang out, and then a *pa-tap, pa-tap, pa-tap* from the side of the stage. Grampa's beat. Ailey found it, then slowly *turned off the radio*. His own taps finding the lead.

> *No brains to think*
> *No beat. No sound.*
> *Crows peckin' away*
> *Oh, can I get down?*
> *As the wind blows*
> *I hope to fall.*
> *Oh, can I win*
> *Oh, can I win at all?*

He didn't have a post, or a box like Mahalia and her swooping crows, but he felt an imaginary stump holding him up like a rag doll. He opened his eyes.

He was the Scarecrow dangling in a field.

> *Up at the top*
> *Stuck on the pole*
> *I ask myself can I wiggle my toes?*
> *My feet to ground is what I seek*
> *And a mind to hope, a mind to think*
> *Oh, can I win*
> *Oh, can I get down?*
> *Oh, can I win*
> *Oh, can I get down?*

When he was ready, his feet did a *ka-clickitty-clickitty-clac* as he broke free of his imaginary post. He stumbled forward, missing a step. But he quickly found it again. He tapped to the left of the stage and then the right.

> *Finally free, finally free*
> *Free from these crows pecking at me.*
> *I'm finally free, I'm finally free*
> *To live and think and tap my feet*
> *What a beautiful sound*
> *What a beautiful beat.*

Words flowed from his throat, and his feet padded across the stage as if each word and each sound were imprinted on him through practice. He no longer faltered or stumbled. As sure as there were stars in the night sky, he had this.

Although he couldn't sing like Mahalia, he gave it his best, sprinkled with something unexpected. Not only could he tap like thunder, his rhyme sparkled. He didn't need Mahalia's glitter.

Bojangles's taps glimmered under the auditorium lights. By the time he rapped: *That's right, that's right. You can't get out of the game*—his final lines, everyone, especially the other Scarecrows in the first few rows clapped and danced along. Even Mahalia was out of her seat.

Ailey slid to a stop, panting. He'd left it all on the stage.

"Nicely done." Ms. Hansberry vaulted from her seat. Her dress whirling around her. "You definitely put a twist on the original."

Ailey's breaths came short and quick. He couldn't speak, but his smile stretched from ear to ear.

"Tapping and rapping aren't in the original *Wiz*, but we might just find a place for them in ours," she added.

Ailey's head flung back. "Wait, does that mean I got the part?"

"Whoa, not so fast," she said. "There were a lot of wonderful auditions. You'll just have to wait, like everyone else." She motioned toward the seats.

Instead of going back to the audience though, Ailey raced to the side of the stage. The curtains swung. Grampa was gone. His head drooped a little and he made his way down the stairs, searching.

Classmates gave him energetic high-fives as he passed. And Ailey relished the attention. He'd done it. Even though he didn't see Grampa, he smiled because they'd both kept their part of the deal.

Whatever happened next was up to the stars and Ms. Hansberry.

CHAPTER FORTY-THREE

A SMIDGEN OF YOUR OWN MAGIC

After what felt like an eternity, Ms. Hansberry took center stage. Some parents had slipped into the back rows. But there was still no Grampa.

"So that we can all go home and rest up for tomorrow's rehearsal . . ." Ms. Hansberry ruffled a sparkly silver paper over her head. "Here it is."

A murmur swept through the auditorium. Everyone shifted in the seats.

"Now before we let you know the cast, remember we have roles for all our stars. So, nobody should go away feeling disappointed or discouraged. This production won't be possible without each one of my brilliant and talented darlings. So, without further ado . . ." She held the paper in front of her.

Ailey leaned forward in his seat, then crashed back against the wood chair hard, biting his bottom lip.

"Drum roll, please," Ms. Hansberry asked.

All the students lifted imaginary drumsticks and revved their tongues against the roofs of their mouths. *Babrummm-brrum.*

"Sissieretta Jones will star as none other than our spectacular Wicked Witch. Juano Hernandez will play the Tin Man. Our Cowardly Lion will be Maceo Merriweather."

Maceo hopped up and let out a roar, clawing the air. Everyone erupted into laughter except Ailey, who squeezed his hands together.

Please, oh please, oh please.

"Canada Lee will become the Wizard . . ." Ailey couldn't bear to hear anymore. He just wanted to know his name was next to "Scarecrow." But the longer he waited, the more doubts he had. He was certain Mahalia's name would be called.

He sat with his head down, flicking at his watchband.

"And our Scarecrow will be played by Ailey Lane."

Ailey didn't move.

"Ailey, that's you." Maceo shoved him. "Ailey, you're the Scarecrow. You got the part!"

Ailey suddenly felt like a million hands shook him.

"Wait, what?" It took him a second to realize what Maceo said. When he did, Ms. Hansberry was already announcing Mahalia as Dorothy.

"Huh?" Mahalia shouted, jumping up. "But I'm supposed

to be the Scarecrow! He didn't even sing that well. And there's no tapping or rapping in *The Wiz*."

"Have a seat, Mahalia," Ms. Hansberry said in her sternest teacher voice. "Ailey gave an excellent audition, and so did you. We want to give everyone's talent the opportunity to shine. And besides, it's okay to change things up a bit. Keeps us unique."

Energy and excitement hurdled through Ailey. The two-ton brick that'd been plopped on his chest all weekend smashed to the ground. He'd done it. He couldn't believe it, he, Ailey Benjamin Lane, had really done it!

As commotion kicked up around him, he bent forward, peering at his feet. He could just make out the outline of the straw hat in the shine of the shoes. "We did it," he whispered. "We did it!"

He felt invincible. Like his Black Panther.

And the only one he wanted to celebrate the news with right then was Grampa.

Ailey stood, searching the room again, while everyone else hugged and jumped around. Grampa stood by the last row.

Their eyes locked. Then Grampa's gaze shifted to the stage and back at Ailey. Ailey's cheeks pushed up so far, he almost couldn't see. He dashed the rest of the way up the aisle, crashing into Grampa's arms. "We did it, Grampa. We did it!"

"No, *you* did it, Jackrabbit." Grampa corrected.

"With the help of friends, wishes, and stars," Ailey added, excited.

"And determination, courage, practice, and *grit*."

"And family," Ailey said. "Don't forget family." One of the shoelaces unraveled and drooped to the side. "Oh yeah, and I can't forget a smidgen of magic." Ailey wiggled the shoe.

"And a smidgen of *your own* magic," Grampa added, clapping his back. Then he leaned close to Ailey's ear. "Even in Harlem, you had your very own magic. You shined there too. And helped me change my stars."

Ailey squeezed Grampa tight and peeked down at the shoes. They sparkled like twinkling stars.

"We did it," Ailey whispered. "All of us. Together."

BLACK EXCELLENCE LIST

Notable Names & Places in
THE MAGIC IN CHANGING YOUR STARS

Did you recognize any of the characters' names? Did some of them sound somewhat familiar? That's because the characters in this story were named after famous Black individuals—dancers, designers, scientists, authors, politicians. Here's a bit of history about real people and places that personify Black Excellence.

Alvin Ailey—January 5, 1931–December 1, 1989
Dancer, choreographer, director, activist, and founder of the highly successful Alvin Ailey American Dance Theater.

Benjamin Banneker—November 9, 1731–October 9, 1806
Astronomer, mathematician, surveyor, almanac author, inventor, writer, and farmer. Important intellectual.

Bill "Bojangles" Robinson—May 25, 1878–November 25, 1949
Dancer, actor, activist. A household name, he was the most famous and highest paid Black entertainer of his time.

Mahalia Jackson—October 26, 1911–January 27, 1972
Gospel singer and civil rights activist. Known as an "early influencer," she was inducted into the Rock & Roll Hall of Fame in 1997.

Lorraine Hansberry—May 19, 1930–January 12, 1965
Playwright and author. First African American woman to have a play on Broadway.

John S. Rock—October 13, 1825–December 3, 1866
Grammar school teacher, dentist, physician, lawyer, abolitionist, and orator. First African American to obtain a medical degree and the first African American lawyer admitted to practice at the U.S. Supreme Court.

Francis Coppin—January 8, 1837–January 21, 1913
Teacher, lecturer, missionary, and principal. Born enslaved in Washington, DC, she became the first African American female school principal.

Josephine Baker—June 3, 1906–April 12, 1975
Dancer, singer, civil rights activist, and French Resistance agent. An extremely popular entertainer in France, she was also the first African American to star in a major motion picture.

Billie Holiday—April 7, 1915–July 17, 1959
Jazz singer. Considered one of the greatest jazz singers of all time.

Sammy Langford—March 4, 1883–January 12, 1956
Once called the "Greatest Fighter Nobody Knows." He was a well-respected heavyweight boxer, who first lost sight in his left eye, but continued boxing for eight years until his career ended because of complete blindness.

Aida Overton Walker—February 14, 1880–October 11, 1914
Vaudeville performer, actress, dancer, singer, and choreographer. Known as "The Queen of the Cakewalk," a popular dance.

Jan Ernest Matzeliger—September 15, 1852–August 24, 1889

Inventor. In 1883, he created a shoe-lasting machine that made it possible to create up to 700 pairs of shoes daily instead of the 50 that were often made by hand. This invention revolutionized shoe-making.

Jupiter Hammon—October 17, 1711–1806.

Writer. Considered one of the founders of African American literature. The first published African American poet.

Zelda Wynn Valdes—June 28, 1905–September 26, 2001

Fashion designer and costumer who owned a boutique called "Chez Zelda" and catered to an elite celebrity clientele.

Sojourner Truth—1797–November 26, 1883

Women's rights activist, abolitionist, writer, and evangelist. Throughout her life she toured, speaking out against injustice in many forms.

Maceo Merriweather—March 31, 1905–February 23, 1953

Pianist and singer. Inducted into the Blues Hall of Fame in 2002.

King "Rastus" Brown—1880s–1940s

Tap dancer. A legendary "Buck and Wing" dancer.

James Van Deer Zee—June 29, 1886–May 15, 1983

Photographer, violinist, and pianist. Active during the Harlem Renaissance and known for photographing Black New York.

Bumpy Johnson—October 31, 1905–July 7, 1968

Mob boss and bookmaker in Harlem (not really Black Excellence, but a noted historical figure).

Asa Philip Randolph—April 15, 1889–May 16, 1979
Civil rights and labor activist. Key organizer in the first predominately African American labor union, the Brotherhood of Sleeping Car Porters.

Franny Criss—1866–February 2, 1942
Dressmaker. Known for her handmade gowns for an elite clientele.

Henry Armstrong—December 12, 1912–October 24, 1988
Professional boxer and heavyweight champion.

Jack Johnson—March 31, 1878–June 10, 1946
Professional boxer. First African American to win the World Heavyweight Championship.

Joe Louis—May 13, 1914–April 12, 1981
Professional boxer. Heavyweight champion for a record twelve years. One of the most successful boxers of all time.

Juano Hernandez—July 19, 1896–July 17, 1970
Afro-Puerto Rican stage and film actor, singer, and amateur boxer.

Edwina "Salt" Evelyn—September 19, 1922–
Tap dancer. Part of the Salt & Pepper tap duo with her sister, Jewel "Pepper" Welch.

Jewel "Pepper" Welch—1922–April 21, 1992
Tap dancer. Part of the Salt & Pepper tap duo with her sister, Edwina "Salt" Evelyn.

Abram Petrovich Gannibal—1696–May 14, 1781
Highly educated African-born military engineer, general, and Russian nobleman. Raised as godson to emperor Peter the Great.

Paul Cuffe—January 17, 1759–September 7, 1817
Businessman, philanthropist, sea captain, whaler, merchant, and abolitionist. He became one of the wealthiest African Americans in the U.S.

Madam CJ Walker—December 23, 1867–May 25, 1919
Businesswoman, philanthropist, and social and political activist. A self-made millionaire, she was one of the wealthiest African American women of her time.

Ann Lowe—December 14, 1898–February 25, 1981
Fashion designer. Well-known couturiere who designed the wedding dress of future First Lady Jacqueline Kennedy when she married John F. Kennedy.

Robert Robinson Taylor—June 8, 1868–December 13, 1942
Architect and educator. One of the first African American architects and the first African American student at Massachusetts Institute of Technology.

Maurice Ellis—May 11, 1905–January 25, 2003
A highly sought after radio voice actor whose skills allowed him to play a wide range of roles (including those intended for whites) for characters of "19 to 70 years of age."

Jarena Lee—February 11, 1783–February 3, 1864
Preacher and author. First female preacher of the African Methodist Episcopal Church of America.

Sissieretta Jones—January 5, 1868 or 1869–June 24, 1933
Opera singer. First African American to headline at Carnegie Hall.

Canada Lee—March 3, 1907–May 9, 1952
Actor, musician, jockey, boxer, and civil rights activist. A leading African American actor of his time.

DRINKING GOURD—The Big Dipper. Many enslaved people followed it to the North Star (Polaris) to know the direction to freedom in the North.

TREE OF HOPE—A wishing tree that many up-and-coming entertainers rubbed for good luck before going on stage. In the 1920s–1930s, it was located on Seventh Avenue, along what was nicknamed the Boulevard of Dreams. In 1934, half of the stump went to the Apollo Theater, and in 1941, Bojangles Robinson moved a piece of it to Eighth Avenue and 131st Street.

(*Author's note:* Although Mr. Robinson did not dedicate the Tree of Hope until two years after Ailey arrived in Harlem, I'd like to think he would be okay with it appearing a bit earlier in this story—so Ailey and Taps could have a smidgen of luck.)

UPPER DARBY—A small township in Pennsylvania. Also, a noted stop on the Underground Railroad, where thousands of enslaved people in pursuit of freedom found shelter and support by local townspeople.

FORT MOSE (Moh-say)—The first African American town in the United States. Settled in 1738 near St. Augustine, Florida.

HARLEM RENS—New York Renaissance basketball team. In 1939, they became the first all-Black pro team to win a basketball World Championship.

BALTIMORE BLACK SOX—1916-1933 Professional Negro League Baseball team based in Baltimore, Maryland.

LEON'S THRIFTWAY—Grocery store located in Kansas City, Missouri. It is one of the oldest African American grocery stores in the U.S.

HOT MIKADO—A musical theater adaptation of Gilbert and Sullivan's *The Mikado* with an all African American cast, starring Bill "Bojangles" Robinson. A highly popular Broadway musical that went on to be performed at the New York World's Fair in 1939.

BLACK SWAN RECORDS—Jazz and blues record label based in Harlem. One of the first African American owned and operated record labels.

TAKE THE "A" TRAIN—Jazz song written in 1939 by Billy Strayhorn. Made famous by Duke Ellington and His Orchestra.

APOLLO THEATER—A popular Harlem venue for many African American performers. It features a famous amateur night.

ACKNOWLEDGMENTS

The words *thank you* feel so inadequate when trying to convey my deepest appreciation and gratitude to all those who have been a part of this journey. To my parents, my guiding stars from the very beginning, you light up any space you enter. Thank you for making sure that I have always seen, heard, and felt Black Excellence all around me and for never tiring of trying to get me to see it within myself. And thank you to my entire family for your unwavering support of me and my dreams.

To the Figments, I'm so lucky to have you ladies in my life and in my corner. Christina, Liza, and Marcie, I appreciate you helping me protect my shine! To all those who have had a hand in this story's journey, I'm grateful. To everyone at Sterling, thank you for rallying around this book and me! Anthony, your warmth is infectious; Hannah, your hope for this story fills my heart; and Suzy, I appreciate your thoughtfulness and keen editorial eye. And thank you for the evening at Alvin Ailey. It was a sparkle of kindness one never expects or even dares to hope for.

To my agent, Clelia Gore, I appreciate you seeing who I

am at my core and for not trying to alter or change that, but for helping coax it out. Thank you! To Mrs. Robinson and Collie Burton, thank you for having answers to my sometimes peculiar questions. And to my Spalding family, thank you for helping me learn to tell better stories. To all the classes, workshop partners, and instructors who have helped make each word I write stronger and more intentional, your imprint is on these pages. To my girls—Cathy, Enola, Christina, Laura, Ibi, Daria, Aida, Kristin, and Alicia—you hold me up, you hold me down, and I am forever grateful for your friendship. I couldn't imagine this journey without each of you. And to Linda Sue, thank you for bringing balance and clarity in so many things and in so many ways.

Mandy Yates, thank you for getting me to write a pitch for a story that only twinkled in my head and heart. Mr. "Bojangles" Robinson, thank you for you! And Alaman Diadhiou. Alaman, like Mr. Robinson, your inspiring taps uplift those you don't even know. Rubin, although I cringe at my own rambles, thank you for patiently listening to me rattle on about my early ideas. E, I appreciate you helping keep my head on (relatively) straight at any hour. Mark, thank you for calling me on all my corny lines and for taking care of my heart like it was your own. And Boston, my furry heart and soul, I can only imagine the knowledge you would drop if you could speak. Thank you for always treating me like a star and for guiding me to this story. You're the best friend a girl could ever ask for, but to me, you are truly so much more than that.

And to Lesléa Newman, whose sparkle instantly lets you know you are in the presence of a brilliant light! If I don't have adequate words to thank my parents, I definitely don't have them to express my thanks to you. From the moment our paths connected, your support and words of encouragement have been a trail of stars. Thank you so much for being a part of changing mine. I will forever be grateful for your belief in me and for your unwavering support of my stories.

And to all those who've ever wished on a star, I hope this book will have you charging toward your possibilities with fists pumping and head held high. Never fear searching out your stars, because the results can be magical!

Thank you!!!!